UNFORGIVEN

LUNA MORADA

Ebook ISBN: 979-8-9888441-0-5

Paperback ISBN: 979-8-9888441-1-2

Hardcover ISBN: 979-8-9888441-2-9

Author's Note: This is a work of fiction. Any names or characters, businesses or places, events or incidents, are fictitious. Any resemblance to actual persons, living or dead, or actual events is purely coincidental.

Cover Design by Firefly Book Covers.

Edited by Simply Spellbound Edits.

CONTENTS

To the child within.
We did it!

FOREWORD

This book contains references to alcohol and drug consumption, domestic violence, anxiety attacks, and explores themes around suicide, generational trauma and addiction.

PROLOGUE

Warmth envelopes me as I rise to my feet. I'm standing in an unfamiliar room. My eyes dart around, looking for the light source and I realize it is coming from the outside.

This room couldn't possibly be so bright just by natural light, but I see that none of the light fixtures are turned on.

To my left, there is an enormous, white marble countertop, at least two inches thick, and what appear to be kitchen cabinets covered with tarp. Directly in front of me are double French doors which are wide open, allowing a warm salty breeze to waft inside. I can smell everything so vividly here. Someone is grilling meat outside, and I also smell grilled fruit—pineapples, green bananas, maybe even coconut.

It smells divine.

I can hear waves crashing right outside the doors.

When did I come to the beach? Whose house am I in?

As I take a couple steps forward, I hear a familiar voice.

"Amor!" he exclaims.

My blood turns cold. Fear resurfaces so quickly, I can hardly breathe.

Just then, he walks past me carrying a bright white marble tile. I stand frozen, unable to control my trembling.

He looks just like I remember him in his youth. Tall and lean with beautifully tanned skin; his head clean shaven to keep him cool while he works, and big ears sticking out the sides. It couldn't *possibly* be him. I haven't seen or spoken to him in over a decade, and that is intentional. Yet, here he stands, healthy and strong, a stark contrast to the last time I saw him.

"How's the floor looking?" he asks.

Confused by his question, I look down at the ground, my eyes now adjusting to the very bright room.

"It looks great, Papi," I say slowly, barely recognizing my child-like voice.

He was a very skilled craftsman. He specialized in flooring and could lay a tile floor down in record time, without ever using spacers. In his prime, he was highly sought out to do custom stone and tile work for very wealthy clients.

"Where are we?"

He smiles. *"You know where we are."*

His smile comforts me, which is unnerving.

This is a dream, but it feels too real. Like I can go right up to him and touch him.

Yeah. I'm not trying that.

But there is no other logical explanation. This *must* be a dream. I should really stop eating dairy before bed.

"I wasn't expecting you today, Hija, but now that you're here, you can help me finish up."

Nodding in agreement, I remind myself that I am perfectly safe. I kneel beside him while he spreads some thin set across the floor.

He looks so real, but I am scared to touch him. I have so many questions, but I'm scared to ask them.

His smirk tells me he knows I'm uncomfortable. He finds this knowledge entertaining.

"I'm very happy here," he assures me.

I slowly nod, taking in my surroundings. "This place does feel very peaceful."

He smiles again. "Oh, yes, quiet too. The voices are gone."

He lays the marble tile down perfectly.

"You used to hear voices?" I ask, my eyes bulging.

He doesn't respond. Instead, he instructs me to grab another tile and hold it for him until he is ready. I repeat this a few more times until he announces that we've finished.

He stands back and seems to admire his work.

It looks great, like always, but his expression is one of . . . wonder. Like he can't believe what he is seeing.

"Why are you looking at the floor like that?" I ask.

He looks up at me, and I see something I'd never witnessed before. Something foreign and what I always thought impossible.

I wince, suddenly feeling exposed and vulnerable.

His eyes are so full of . . . life! They glow in the most vibrant shade of brown and dance with excitement.

It felt as if I was staring into the depths of Earth's richest soil; dark, strong, and ready to fortify.

"I'm not looking at the floor like anything," he says gently.

He then points back at the glossy marble. It was then, I noticed a reflection.

My reflection.

"I'm looking at you."

1

BEGINNING OF THE END

"Emilia, this isn't like you. Talk to me. Why have you been so distant?"

I'm tired. Bored and uninspired. You've neglected me for years, and now I've realized that I don't want your attention anymore. I want to fall in love again someday . . . I haven't been in love with you in a very long time.

I lack the courage to utter those words. "Nathan, I want a divorce."

He squeezed my hand harder. He stiffened as his eyes welled up with tears. "No."

"Nathan, I—"

"Em, NO."

"I've already made my deci—"

"No. I love you, and I can fix this. I'll go back to therapy. I promise it's not as bad as it looks. I'm not letting go. I can't. You're all I have."

Tears rolled down his face, yet I couldn't bring myself to feel bad.

To feel anything . . .

"Come on Nate, let's be honest. You've been sad for a *very* long time, and I've had to be a fly on the wall for all of it. I'm tired. I can't keep wasting away in a loveless marriage while you try to figure yourself out, and I hope you'll notice I'm here."

"Loveless?" He recoiled like he'd been slapped across the face.

"Nate, I want this to end as painlessly as possible."

"You don't love me anymore?" he asked, the defeated look in his eyes beginning to break my resolve.

I stared into his beautiful, wet, brown eyes. I remembered the day I fell madly in love with those eyes. We were so young and hopeful. We had promised each other the world.

Those eyes now looked so tired.

So scared.

We got married twenty years ago. Once Nate completed his bachelor program, we relocated to North Carolina from Long Island, New York, so he could go to law school. I'd worked as a hair stylist for the last seventeen years, and while helping women feel beautiful and rejuvenated was fun, the job came with pitfalls.

My clients had all sorts of wonderful tales about their travels, romantic getaways with their spouses, and all their children's milestones. One time, a client came in for a bridal hair trial. I had just seen her two weeks prior for her regular trim, and she was still a happily single woman then. Apparently, she had met the man of her dreams on a girl's trip to Cancun, and two weeks later they were planning their elopement on an Alpaca farm.

Who the hell gets married on an Alpaca farm?

All these adventures, none of which I could relate to . . . Each day that passed, I grew more restless.

More stuck.

"Em, please don't make any final decisions right now. If you want space, that's fine, you got it. You won't even know I'm here. But please, just give me a chance. This is too sudden after twenty years of marriage. Why don't we just separate for a while . . . six months! Just give me six months. Please?"

Can six months really undo years of unhappiness? I don't think so.

Nevertheless, he had a point. It wouldn't be fair to deny him time to process and, hopefully, accept our new reality.

"Fine. Six months, but I'm still leaving, Nate. I put in my notice at work. I'm going back home."

"To Long Island?" he asked, clearly perplexed. "I figured you'd still be local. I hoped I'd at least get to see you." I noticed the familiar look of withdrawal spread across his face.

Nate held nothing but disdain for our hometown, which was precisely the reason I had decided to go. I knew he wouldn't try to follow me.

"No, Nate. I need a change of scenery," I sighed.

"Can we talk? Can I call you?"

"I . . . I don't think that's a good idea," I responded.

"Fine. Can I write you?"

Huh?

"That way you don't feel obligated to respond, unless you want to of course."

"Okay." My look of puzzlement was obvious. I wouldn't describe Nate as a "letter writing" type of guy.

"Emilia, please. P*lease* don't give up on me."

I gave him a weak smile and got up to leave. As I grabbed my keys and headed to my packed car, I turned around and looked at his tear-stricken face one more time.

How has he not realized that I gave up on him years ago?

The drive from North Carolina to Long Island is about ten hours without traffic, and while that may seem daunting to some, I enjoyed it. I've driven plenty of times before, for holidays, weddings, birthday parties, and really any social event with my family. Nate was never interested in joining me for these events. Sure, I could have just hopped a plane to JFK, but I just loved the idea of having ten hours to myself.

This road trip's playlist featured a wide variety: 80s Ballads, 90s grunge, Mariachi, and a whole lot of Selena—Yes! She *is* her own genre, because every musical style she interpreted was instantly elevated, and I will die on that hill. Another perk of riding long distances alone . . . my Volvo became a safe space where I could wail to my heart's content.

Although Nate and I are both Hispanic, only I speak Spanish, so listening to Spanish music always felt awkward around him. Nate's stepfather was not embracing of his wife's heritage, so Nate never got the opportunity to learn about his roots.

I also had an audiobook to entertain me while my vocal cords recovered, and lastly, a true crime podcast guaranteed to keep me on the edge of my seat during the last leg of the trip.

Given my current mental state, I opted for a more scenic route through the mountains. As I hopped on I-77 North, I started to notice the twinge of guilt in my stomach. I knew Nate would struggle emotionally without me there. I was always "his rock."

And that's just it. I am not a rock.

I, too, had ambitions and dreams. I, too, have had my share of sorrows in life. Unlike him, I never had anyone to call "my rock."

Not even a pebble.

Our early troubles bonded us as teenagers. We both came from broken homes where mayhem was dished out like a daily meal. When we met in high school, I was surprised that this handsome, yet quiet guy didn't already have a girlfriend.

It wasn't from lack of admirers. Nate was of average height with brown hair that he wore medium length, and warm brown eyes that weren't quite light enough to be hazel. He had broad shoulders and a muscular build, but no one was sure what he did to stay fit, since he didn't participate in any sports. He didn't seem to have many friends; again not because people didn't try to talk to him, he just didn't engage. His younger brother, Jonathan, was a freshman at our high school, and they usually sat together at lunch.

Nate never seemed interested in anything, except for our government and politics class. He and I had several classes together, but this was the only subject where he was an active participant, and he was top of our class.

One day, we were paired together for a project, and I had to pry every word out of him during the first thirty minutes. Once he relaxed, his intelligence shined through. He had a lot of depth, especially for a kid his age.

It didn't take long for us to grow close.

Nate says I've always been easy to talk to. I'd heard that before, but I always had ulterior motives. I was a good listener when it came to other people's stories and experiences, because it offered an escape from my reality.

I was raised in a single parent household. My mom was the ultimate provider. As an immigrant from Central America, that little woman worked two, sometimes three jobs to support me, which, unfortunately, meant that she was rarely home. At that time, I didn't consider my mom very affectionate, but I still felt loved. Even though I spent most of my time home alone, I always had a home cooked meal, a roof over my head, and clean clothes. That was more than she ever got as a kid.

Our relationship soured a bit in my teen years. I resented that the little time she did have outside of work was spent fighting with her then boyfriend. He was okay, I guess, except for when he was cheating on her and blaming her for his excursions. There were a lot of heated arguments in the house, which sometimes turned violent.

My father was absent most of the time, yet he managed to inflict more damage on me in those short cameo appearances than anyone ever had.

Nate became my escape. When he finally confided in me about his stepfather's violent outbursts, especially toward his mom, I let my guard fall easily.

I thought I was the only one with screwed up parents . . .

In English, we always sat in the back corner of the classroom. Our class knew we were an item, even though he was never outwardly affectionate.

One day, shortly before graduation, he walked into class and sat in his usual spot next to me.

"Beautiful," he greeted me with a nod.

I always deflected his sweet words to hide my emotions. "Ah, Lord Nathan! How kind of you to join me on this marvelous day," I responded.

He rolled his eyes while a sexy smirk spread across his face. "I got you a birthday gift, but I won't let you open it until we get to my place," he teased.

In the afternoons, I'd go to Nate's place after school and do homework, among other things, until his parents got home.

"Why tell me that you got me a gift if you weren't going to let me open it?" I asked.

"To torture you," he said, matter-of-factly.

"I see. Well, since our birthdays are only two days apart, I also got you a gift. Being that I am the superior half of this relationship, I'll let you open it now."

He chuckled.

I slowly put his gift box on the table and slid it over, making sure not to disrupt the teacher. He made a show of covertly bringing the box behind the table and placing it on his lap.

As he popped the jewelry box open, I saw his big brown eyes light up. He pulled out the class ring and examined it. It was made of white gold and had an emerald gemstone. I knew his parents wouldn't make an effort to celebrate his graduation.

But he *deserved* it.

Despite all the bullshit he went through at home, he was still graduating with honors and a near perfect GPA.

"Where did you get the money for this?" he asked as he slipped the ring on his right finger. It fit perfectly, a lucky guess on my part.

"I sold a kidney," I replied as I lifted the back of my shirt.

I had amassed an impressive fortune for a girl my age. I had begun saving Christmas, birthday, and summer job money for my first car.

"I love it," he whispered. Then he brought his left hand to mine and held me the remainder of class.

When we got to Nate's house, he told me to make myself comfortable while he whipped up our regular Friday dinner— ramen noodles with eggs.

I taught him how to doctor up ramen noodle soup using potatoes, green bananas, eggs, and a dash of hot sauce and lime, which is how I grew up eating it. Nate didn't grow up eating a lot of Hispanic food. His stepfather always complained about the taste, so his mom cooked bland food. One time, he served me some leftover pasta she'd made. It looked like pasta, but it tasted like tap water.

They didn't have any veggies in the house, so we had it egg drop style. We both sat cross-legged on his full-size mattress slurping away at our noodles while listening to "Something in the Way" by Nirvana.

This was our safe space.

When we finished eating, he reached into his backpack and pulled out the gift bag.

I reached out to take the bag from him, but he pulled it back out of my reach.

"Hold on. when you open it, I want you to hear me out before responding."

I nodded anxiously and opened the bag. I pulled out the jewelry box, giggling at the irony of us both choosing jewelry for this year's gift. Inside, was a dainty silver heart necklace with a little emerald stone in the center. I began to coo when he stopped me.

"I didn't only choose emerald because it's your birth stone, but for its significance. Emerald is said to represent rebirth and renewal. So far, our home life has been shit. We turn eighteen in a few days and can quite literally choose to not be here anymore. I want us to become something new. I'm going to become a lawyer so I can give us decent life. If you'll have me?"

I felt the tears well up inside me. Until then, I hadn't really thought about all the freedom and possibilities adulthood would bring.

"Emilia, will you marry me?"

I giggled. "You got it. When?" I asked as I put my necklace on.

"Monday."

I froze and stared up at him, my eyes coming out of their sockets.

"You want to get married . . . in three days?" I slowly repeated.

"I know we're young, but I could never picture a day without you in it. You're my best friend," he said softly. "I'm in love with you."

I straddled him and gave him the fiercest hug I could muster. "Okay, then let's get married in three days," I whispered to him as I looked into his gorgeous eyes.

That beautiful smirk of his reappeared, and he kissed me. It was the most passionate kiss I'd ever experienced. Then, he made love to me. Once we had finished, we held each other until his alarm went off signaling it was time for me to go home. After several more kisses, I said my goodbyes.

As I jumped into the shower, I realized I too, had never felt safe unless I was with him. I closed my eyes and felt the warm water flow down my body. I felt loved. I felt safe.

That was a first.

That version of Nate lasted a few more years. We married at a courthouse the following Monday. Nate and I graduated the following week, and, as expected, there was no celebration waiting for us. We didn't let it get us down. He and I made our plans and hit the ground running.

Nate began college in the fall and took every class he could, grinding to finish his four-year program in two. I took a job at a pharmaceutical factory to support us while he studied. He was a fantastic husband, lover, and housemate. Nate, I quickly learned, was an insomniac, averaging no more than four or five hours of sleep a night. He would study while I slept, then get up, pack us lunch, and wake me up in the sexiest of ways, all before sunrise.

When we got home in the evenings, we'd clean our small one-bedroom apartment together, and then he'd study at the breakfast counter while I made us dinner. There was no more yelling or screaming . . . no fights or cries of pain because someone was getting beat up.

Just two people in love, trying to make our dreams come true.

As soon as Nate graduated, he was accepted into a law school in North Carolina. Our parents were still resentful of our decision to marry so young, and Jonathan had enlisted in the Air Force, so we didn't have a reason to stay. We packed our belongings and moved down south. He began law school, and I enrolled in cosmetology school.

That's when it happened.

Nate's passion turned into obsession. His already short sleep cycle dwindled to one or two hours. He was constantly irritable, and whatever time he had outside of schoolwork was spent looking for internships. I tried to remain patient, but I was juggling work and school. I tried to build our savings so we could move out of our two-bedroom apartment.

Although the romance had begun to fizzle, our relationship was nothing like what we had experienced as kids. In fact, things turned around, albeit temporarily.

There I stood in our bathroom one morning, in a t-shirt and underwear, staring down at a positive pregnancy test.

I . . . got . . . pregnant. While on birth control.

I was terrified. I knew Nate would be pissed because of our derailed plans.

I didn't even get a moment to figure out how I'd break the news. I had forgotten he didn't have class and was still home. When he came in to brush his teeth, he startled me, and I let out a blood curdling scream. He chuckled at my horrified reaction and grabbed me by the sides of the face.

"Baby, relax. Jeez, you look like you just saw a ghost."

I slowly peeked at the counter, and he followed my gaze down to the pregnancy test.

When he saw it, he picked it up and read the result.

"Pregnant," he read slowly.

He looked back at me wide-eyed, not saying anything.

"I don't know how it happened. I swear I've been taking my birth control on time. I've been under a lot of stress lately, maybe birth control isn't effective if I'm stressed out? Nate? Say something!"

He blinked slowly a couple of times and then wrapped me in his arms, just about squeezing the life out of me. He held me for what seemed like ages before putting a hand on my flat stomach.

"Our baby . . ." he whispered in wonder, before looking up at me with eyes full of tears.

I relaxed and smiled, all my worry washing away.

———

The joy and laughter only lasted a couple of months. One day at a routine checkup, I was notified that our baby's heart was no longer beating. Nate hadn't accompanied me to the visit, so I sat with that shit all alone for hours until he got home, and we could discuss.

He walked in the door with a bag from the pharmacy, likely full of candy bars and gummy bears. He always loved tending to my cravings. I was coiled up on the couch and he rushed towards me, concern in his eyes.

When I broke the news, I felt numb. It all felt so surreal. Nate was clearly heartbroken, but I just sat there comforting him while silently wondering why I couldn't feel anything. I knew I was sad. I knew it would eventually hit me, but in the moment, I just felt nothing.

He hugged and kissed me and told me we would get through this. The next day, we went to the clinic to pick up my prescription. Later that day I experienced the worst pain I had ever felt.

He caressed my back while I writhed in pain, and told me he loved me repeatedly while I cried into my pillow.

Everything continued to spiral. I became obsessed with getting pregnant again. I felt like my body had failed me. Like I had killed our baby. After the second and third miscarriage, however, I realized I wasn't meant to bring children into this world.

The added stress did nothing but amplify Nate's anxiety and his grades began to suffer. The more anxious he became, the longer his periods of isolation would stretch. I tried to hold down the fort while he processed his emotions, but as the years passed, I realized there was no "processing" happening.

Nathan was in full shutdown mode.

He flunked the Bar exam twice. When his internship yielded no opportunities, he retreated to our nursery. He eventually landed a role at an insurance company. It offered more financial security, and he quickly climbed the corporate ladder, but his hours were long, and we hardly saw each other. When I tried to engage with him, he seemed to be annoyed at my mere presence. Conversations between us became robotic.

"How was your day?" "What's for dinner?" "You go, I'll stay home and catch up on sleep."

Staying busy at work helped distract me from my own sadness. Nate and I were hardly intimate anymore; our roommate-hood was in full swing. We barely spoke on his good days and didn't see each other on his bad days. Sometimes he would come up to bed, say good night, and then turn his back.

I was invisible.

Before I knew it, twenty years had passed.

Selena's "Fotos y Recuerdos" had just begun to play on the radio when my sister's ringtone suddenly blared through the car speakers.

I jumped and screamed at the sound, then quickly recovered, and answered. "Hey Flaca, what's going on?"

Raquel is my half-sister on my father's side.

"Emi, where are you?!"

"Uh, I'm going for a drive?" I said, not wanting to explain all the drama happening in my life right now.

"Bullshit. I called Nate because I've been trying to reach you for over an hour, and he's being super evasive."

"Relax, I'm on the highway and may have had some bad reception. Why do you sound so agitated?"

"It's dad, Emi. He's dead," she said, her voice breaking.

"He's not dead," I responded, annoyed. "He's probably just off screwing a new side piece or something. You know he disappears from time to time."

"He was found at a crack house, Emilia. He's dead."

As she sobbed, I also began to cry and tried to press for details. She said she didn't know specifics and needed my help making funeral arrangements for him. I told her that I was on my way up to New York anyway, so I would stop by her place that night.

After a few more somber exchanges, we hung up. I had made my way to a gas station parking lot and looked in the mirror.

I found myself utterly exhausted.

It takes so much energy to fake tears like that, but for my sister, it was necessary.

Truth be told, I felt nothing.

I feel nothing.

2

CHRISTMAS IS OUT THE WINDOW

Suffolk County Police Department—Arrest Record: 1051564

Date: 12/9/1988
Defendant's Name: Pablo Salinas
Victim's Name: Eva Flores

I, Officer Michelle Pease, Badge #5384, attest to the following and state:

At approximately 20:36 hours, I, with several units, responded to a domestic disturbance call at Sunny Terrace Apartments on 34 Main St. Dispatch advised that multiple neighbors reported hearing screams in apartment 1A.

When officers entered the apartment building, they saw a man holding a woman by the hair and shouting in her face; a toddler was present and screaming. Officers apprehended the assailant so EMTs could administer first aid. The victim had swelling and bruising on the left side of her face and her left ear was bleeding.

She was coherent and able to walk. Once the victim was calm, I took her statement as follows:

- The victim, as listed above, states she was in the kitchen of her one-bedroom apartment when she noticed the smell of cigarette smoke. Her daughter, Emilia Salinas, aged three, was in the living room playing by their Christmas tree. She walked down the hallway to the bedroom where she had a window open.
- When she entered the room, the cigarette smell grew stronger, and she noticed the window screen was torn. She suspected her child's father, the assailant, as listed above, was hiding by the window. She called his name several times, when he suddenly entered the apartment through the window, grabbing her by the arm. She managed to break free and ran down the hallway to the living room and the child began to scream.
- There was a struggle in the living room between the assailant and the victim. The child attempted to intervene but was pushed away by the assailant. Once again, the victim broke free, grabbed the child and rushed out of the apartment. She proceeded to knock on all her neighbor's doors.
- The assailant caught up to the pair and spun the victim around. He struck the victim on the side of her head with a closed fist. She was momentarily disoriented, and then he struck her again. He grabbed her hair and began shouting at her. The victim noticed his eyes were bloodshot and suspected he was high on crack cocaine.

She stated that his excessive drug use was the main cause of their separation.

Officers entered the apartment building and swiftly apprehended the assailant. During a body search, a knife was discovered in his back pocket. No drug paraphernalia was found on his person. The assailant was still shouting expletives at the victim as he was placed into the police vehicle.

The victim was visibly shaken and distraught. EMTs recommended the victim be taken to the nearest hospital for a possible ruptured ear drum. When EMTs brought her outside, she caught a glimpse of the assailant and momentarily fainted. EMTs placed her on a stretcher. The child was cleared of any injuries, and officials later placed her in her uncle's care per the victim's instructions.

Charges are as follows:

Count 1: Violation of Domestic Violence Protective Order
Count 2: Breaking and Entering
Count 3: Aggravated Assault in the 2nd Degree
Count 4: Public Intoxication
Count 5: Endangering the Welfare of a Child

I made it to Raquel's house close to midnight and was so ready for bed. I knocked a few times before she opened the door.

"Emi, I was starting worry that something happened to you," she said through her congestion.

She looked haggard. Her eyes were so swollen they could barely open. Raquel had always been very close to our father, for reasons I didn't quite understand, but wouldn't question.

"It's a ten-hour drive, Flaca," I said as I stepped into her living room.

"Yes, but you took eleven," she scolded.

I chuckled. "I did. The car needed gas and I needed food."

"You're right, I'm sorry. This is all too much, and my anxiety is running high." She wiped the tears from her cheeks.

"I understand. But don't worry. I'm here now, and I've got your back. We will get through this together, okay?"

"I love you, Emi." She cried as I embraced her.

I held her until she calmed, then sat on the couch while she reheated a bowl of pasta she had set aside for me. I insisted I wasn't hungry, but Raquel is, and has always been, a stubborn woman.

I may be eight years older, but she was always the domineering sister. As kids, we only saw each other a couple of months out of the year, when my mom sent me to my father's house for summer vacation.

She sat next to me and leaned her head against the couch.

"Emi, do you remember when dad would take us to the beach?" she asked, with a twinkle in her eyes.

"Mhm," I replied in between bites.

"I would always count down the days until you arrived. It was nice to have someone to play with for a change."

"I remember."

"My favorite memories are of us going down to Myrtle Beach. Dad would play with us at the hotel pool, and we'd spend hours playing together in the sand."

"Yeah . . ."

"What's wrong?" she asked, confused at my tone.

"I don't remember those beach trips as fondly . . ."

"What do you mean?"

"Well, I remember Dad playing with us in the pool for like, thirty minutes and then . . . he would disappear. I remember your mom anxiously searching for him in every hotel bar and restaurant. One time, we were out on the strip past midnight, still looking for him, because he took the car keys. She finally gave up and we had to walk over two miles back to the motel, only to realize he'd been passed out drunk on the motel room floor the whole time."

"I don't remember any of that." A defensive tone always creeped into her voice when I spoke negatively about our father.

"You were four or five at the time, and your mom and I tried our best to keep you distracted."

She grew quiet.

As I finished my meal, she collected my dishes. I took my belongings to the guest room and began to settle in.

Raquel owned a small two-bedroom house. She had once shared the home with her mother, who passed away about a year ago. Marta was by no means perfect, but she was a great stepmom to me. My father left her over a decade ago, but she never got over it. She suffered a lot in her life, and always walked with a slump, like there was a literal weight on her shoulders.

Always downcast.

As she aged, her beautiful cocoa-colored skin turned dull. She didn't smile. She barely spoke unless it was to argue with Raquel. She spent her days staring off into space, thinking about God knows what. A few years ago, she was diagnosed with early-onset dementia and declined rather quickly. Marta needed assistance with everyday tasks, and Raquel, being her only child, took on the responsibility of full-time caregiver. In the end, even when she couldn't recognize her own daughter, she would still ask if anyone had seen my father.

Marta's bedroom was now a craft/guest room. The space was warm and cozy with a queen bed on a simple platform frame, soft, pale-yellow walls, and the comforter and window treatments were lilac with flower embroidery. To the right of the bed was a shelf with stacks of puzzles and scrapbooks. To the left was a large window that let in a lot of natural light, and in the corner, sat a rocking chair, likely for Marta, so she could gaze out into the backyard.

I walked over to the full-length mirror on the wall and stared at my reflection for the first time since I'd left home. Most people can't tell that my sister and I are related. I have wavy, dark brown hair that I keep in a short bob, while Raquel keeps her straight, jet-black hair long. While she inherited her height from Marta and my father, I barely stretched to five foot two. I had put on some weight in recent months with all my emotional eating, but I found I liked the way my curves filled out my clothes. I have olive skin like my father, while she has her mother's cocoa complexion. We do however, both have our father's almond-shaped brown eyes.

After a quick shower, I changed into my pajamas. As I looked around the room, I realized this was my first night sleeping as a single woman . . . *ever*.

There was a mix of emotions at that revelation. Disbelief, excitement . . . and a little sadness.

I'd never envisioned life this way, but Nate felt like a weight I needed to shed in order to find myself.

As I plugged my cell phone into the charger, I noticed I had missed a text from Nate.

Hope you made it to NY safely. I love you.

I miss you.

I was going to ignore the message but chastised myself. I would have liked to have known if *he* made it safely.

I made it. Thanks for checking in. Night.

"Is that Nate?" Raquel asked, leaning against the door.

"Yeah," I sighed.

"Emilia, you know I'm not Team Nate or anything, but don't make any rash decisions, okay? You need your space but take your time. Figure out what it is that you want."

I nodded, suddenly feeling exhausted.

"Sis . . . do you mind if I sleep in here with you tonight?" she asked, a blush creeping up her neck.

I smiled and patted the bed next to me.

As a kid, she always insisted on sleeping with me. Back then, I had been grateful to have her in bed with me too. It shielded us from all the bullshit going on around us.

This strangely felt like old times.

Raquel and I sat in her living room and compiled a list of relatives we needed to notify. I was grateful that she had already called our grandmother, whom I avoided at all costs. Her list included our father's sister, Aunt Sara, and an old boss from his masonry days.

My list included a couple of cousins and my mom. I also decided to call Jonathan, Nate's brother, since he lived nearby, and we were once close. Nate and Jonathan drifted apart after our move to North Carolina, and I really missed our friendship. As expected, Jonathan was the most sympathetic, likely since he'd never met my father, and asked for service details. I agreed to text him when I knew more.

In all, we notified eight people.

We could only think of eight people that would want to come pay their respects.

Because Raquel and I were next of kin, we agreed that cremation was best. We felt it was the most affordable and respectful option given the state of his remains.

We agreed that I would cover the funeral expenses. She was relieved. Raquel's savings took a big hit when her mother died. Marta's last wish was to be sent back to her home country to be buried on the family plot.

"Grandma is going to lose her shit, Emi," she said, shaking her head.

"I know, and I don't care. She can submit her grievances in writing," I muttered as I began to run the numbers.

I felt Raquel's stare and could tell she was debating whether to push the subject. She was good at picking her battles and knew my passivity had its limit.

"I found a funeral home that can have him ready for us by Friday."

"Wow. In a couple days? Is that enough time?" I pondered.

"I've already said yes. Besides, Grandma arrives this evening, and everyone else is local."

She ordered the flowers while I designed a memorial card and ordered prints for the next day. Raquel pulled out several photo albums to search for a large picture of my father to frame. She stopped and stared at her family pictures, likely being transported to happier times. After a few crying spells, she finally located the picture she wanted to use.

I didn't bother to look.

"We've accomplished a lot. Shall we go have some dinner?" I asked, ready to get some fresh air.

"I would love that." She smiled.

———

Sara texted us while we were at dinner to let us know she and my grandmother had just landed. Raquel invited them to join us at the restaurant. She declined, and instead, lectured her on how she should have prepared a meal for their arrival.

"It's common sense, Niña," Sara scolded. "Your grandmother is tired, and it would have been nice to go straight to your house so she could eat and rest. But don't worry, we will grab something on our way to the hotel."

"Okay, Tia. I'll make some lunch and you can stop by tomorrow, okay?" Raquel offered.

"Sure. We'll see you then." Sara hung up.

"Why do you let her lecture you like you're still a child, Flaca?" I chided.

"Emi, you know that's just going to blow up in my face. She will start to argue and then Grandma will start crying. I plan to keep the peace for the next couple days, and then they'll be gone."

I noticed she was playing with her food; so much sadness was buried in her furrowed brows. It hit me then. My little sister didn't have the energy to fight with such egos. Raquel had lost both of her parents. They weren't the best parents, but they were all she had had, besides me.

She looked empty.

That realization brought tears to my eyes. Before I knew it, Raquel was on my side of the booth comforting me.

"It's okay, Emi. He's in a better place now."

I nodded. There was no point in correcting her. My tears were for her.

Not him.

The next day, I decided to run a few errands while Raquel cooked lunch.

"Okay, but please be back before they arrive, Emi. I do not want to be alone with them."

"Yes, I'll be back in an hour," I assured her.

While I drove down the street to go to the grocery store, I looked around, admiring the view. Long Island in the fall was always so beautiful. Our small town had tons of old oak trees that turned the most beautiful shades of amber and red.

I stopped by the pharmacy to pick up the prints I had ordered. My order wasn't quite ready, so I browsed the wine section while I waited, internally debating whether I'd need one or two bottles to get me through the day. Just as I decided on two chardonnays, I heard a familiar voice call my name.

I spun around and Jonathan was standing in front of me, a bottle of laundry detergent in his hand. I smiled from ear to ear as I went up to him and gave him a big hug.

"Woman, look at you!" he said with a warm smile.

"I know! It's been what, five years?"

"Longer, I think . . . How are you holding up?" he asked, his face full of concern.

"I'm okay. I'm sorry I forgot to text, my sister and I had a hectic day."

"No worries! Did you finalize a date?"

"Yes, it's tomorrow."

"Wow, that was quick huh . . . Did Nate come up with you?" he asked, a hopeful gleam in those familiar brown eyes.

Jonathan and Nathan both looked a lot like their mother, except Jonathan was much taller.

But they both had the same gorgeous eyes.

"No, Jon. Eh, Nate and I separated."

Jonathan was clearly taken aback. "Really? When?"

"As of two days ago, actually. I was already making my way up here when Raquel broke the news about my father."

"Man, I'm so sorry, Em. This is a lot to handle in such a short period of time. Still, Nate should be here to support you."

"He doesn't know about my father yet. I asked him for space, so it felt weird to call him a day later, ya know?"

"I suppose. Well, if you need anything, please let me know. If not, I'll see you tomorrow," he said, while he gave me another hug.

Just then my order was called. "Oh wait! I'll give you a card, it has the funeral home address."

He smiled at me and took the card. As he walked away, I felt this gnawing in my gut. I missed that smile so much. It was how Nate used to smile. I shook the feeling off and paid for my items.

The nostalgia was replaced with dread as soon as I pulled into my sister's driveway. There was a car parked, which I assumed was Sara's rental.

An hour early. Figures.

I grabbed the bags and went inside. The house smelled of fresh corn tortillas and my favorite, Sopa de Frijol, a red bean soup made with herbs and vegetables. It smelled amazing. I walked into the kitchen and put the groceries away when my sister called out to me from the backyard. My grandmother, Sara, and Raquel were lounging in the backyard under her pergola.

"Hola, Abuela," I said as I reached down and gave her a hug. She looked so frail compared to the last time I had seen her, almost ten years ago, at a wedding.

"Aha, Mija, how are you?" Her joyful tone made my skin crawl.

"I'm doing well," I said as I reached over to hug Sara. "Tia."

"Hey, Chica," she said with a loose hug.

We made small talk for a few minutes, but everything felt . . . off. You could cut the tension with a knife. There was a lot to be said. I knew both my grandmother and Sara were resentful about my lack of interest in their lives. I had my reasons, and I was happy to discuss them, but I knew they'd never ask. They'd just talk about it amongst themselves.

I looked over to Raquel, whose expression told me they'd been prying, and she'd stalled as long as possible.

"Abuela was just asking about the funeral plans," she said while giving me the "I told you" look.

"Ah, yes. Well, he is being cremated and the service is tomorrow," I said, matter-of-factly.

"WHAT?!" Sara shouted, as my grandmother's mouth fell

open. "What do you mean, he is being cremated? We never agreed to that, we're Catholic for God's sake!"

"I mean what I said." My taunt had its desired effect. Sara looked ready to pounce, and I *really* hoped she would.

Seriously, if looks could kill . . .

Raquel jumped in. "When they found Dad, he had already been gone for a few days, Tia. We wouldn't be able to have an open casket. Besides, the Vatican lifted their ban on cremation a long time ago."

My grandmother stared at me with a look I couldn't quite decipher.

Sara's eyes narrowed. "That is no excuse. We do not cremate in this family. You should have waited on us to arrive so your grandmother could decide what to do with HER son."

Limit reached.

I interjected. "According to the medical examiner, WE are HIS remaining descendants and therefore, the next of kin. So, WE decide what happens with his remains."

"I don't know what your problem is, but it would serve you well to watch your tone," Sara scathed. "You have not been a member of this family for over twenty years, and now you want to call the shots?"

"I'm not calling the shots because I'm family, but because I'm footing the bill."

"Okay, enough!" my grandmother shouted.

We all remained silent while she composed herself.

"What's done is done. If he is cremated, then I at least get to keep him with me," she said, her voice breaking.

Sara added, "The Vatican may allow for cremation, but his ashes cannot be scattered. My mother will be keeping his urn."

I was clenching my jaw so hard I could feel my heartbeat through my teeth.

Raquel's patience seemed to have run out as well. "We selected three small urns. Abuela will get one, Emilia and I will get the other two."

"That is fine," my grandmother said.

"Mama! You should have—"

"I said it is *fine*, Sara." Her tone was final.

Sara looked away for a moment, then yanked her bag off the table. "I am not going to sit here and break bread where I am clearly not welcome. Mama, text me when you are ready, and I'll come get you." She walked away without saying another word.

My grandmother closed her eyes and took a deep breath. When she opened them, I realized she had been holding in a lot of emotions around Sara. "Your father was my only boy. He may not have been a perfect man, but he tried his best."

That was bullshit, but I kept silent.

"I tried everything I could to help him overcome his addiction, but God saw fit to take him, and I will not argue with God's timing."

Raquel and I both surrounded my grandmother and held her as she wept.

Lunch was delicious, and I just about scarfed it down. Raquel brought out her domino set, and our grandmother showed us her gaming skills.

"How is your husband?" she asked me as she laid down her last domino and won yet another round.

Raquel grumbled as she shuffled the dominos. She had a mean competitive streak and was not happy to have lost three times in a row.

"He's okay, Abuela," I said, not wanting to look up at her. I am naturally quick-witted. I can handle small talk all day.

But I could not stomach small talk with *her*. She never cared what I had to say before, why start now?

Before we knew it, it was nighttime, and my grandmother left with Sara. I was in the kitchen cleaning up when Raquel slumped into a stool at the island.

"That was exhausting," she said.

"Beyond. Wine?" I offered as I refilled my glass.

She nodded. While she sipped, I went back to the dishes.

"Emi, why do you take Tia's bait?"

"It's not bait, Flaca. It's disrespect. She thinks herself a commander," I huffed as I furiously scrubbed a pan.

"It's both, Sis. And you walked right into it. Then she spins it around like we are the unreasonable ones. A classic bait and switch."

I stopped scrubbing and burst out laughing. "That's not what a bait and switch is."

"Yes, it is!"

After I explained what that term actually meant, she looked even more confused.

"Okay, well you have to admit that what I said should also be defined as a bait and switch."

We were awake before sunrise to get ready for the nine a.m. service. I couldn't find anything black to wear in my luggage, so Raquel let me borrow a black mini dress she had in her closet. Due to our difference in height, it fell modestly to my knees. Due to our difference in weight, it was a little too tight, so I paired it with an oversized black cardigan and some boots. Physically, I felt fine. Emotionally, I was overwhelmed. I had woken up to a text from Nate.

Jon texted me last night. He told me that your father passed away.
Know that I love you, and I'm here for you if you need anything.

I scoffed at the message. Why the sudden effort? I decided not to respond and called my mom instead. She lived about an hour away but wanted to come pay her respects.

"Mami, just be prepared. Abuela and Sara are here."

"Okay, and?" she asked, her tone very clearly reminding me she didn't care.

"You can be . . . a little combative. Just try to keep your cool, okay?" I warned.

"I can behave like an adult, Emi. It's them you should warn."

"I think I said enough yesterday . . ."

"Oh?" she asked, her interest piqued.

I told her all about the Sara ordeal.

"I don't understand what her problem is," she said.

"I do. She never got along with her brother and doesn't want to be here. Can you blame her?"

"Not one bit."

It was short drive to the funeral home. As we made our way into the viewing room, I decided I didn't want a funeral when I died. The music, the dim lighting, the drapes, the carpeting . . . It was all so drab and depressing.

Toward the front stood the two flower wreaths we had ordered.

Raquel walked up to the front and placed our father's picture frame on the table. The picture she chose wasn't one I'd seen before, but for some reason gave me major déjà vu. He was standing tall in his work clothes with hands on his hips, his head clean shaven to keep him cool while he worked, and big ears sticking out the sides.

On the table, there was an ornamental chest in which the funeral directors had placed the small urns.

My grandmother and Sara had already arrived and were sitting in the front row. It was clear my grandmother was crying, while Sara mindlessly rubbed her back. His old boss came by and left flowers, then a few cousins came by and gave my grandmother a hug. They invited her to their house after the service, which she agreed to, much to our relief. Raquel and I declined the invitation, feigning exhaustion.

Just then, my mom walked in with Jonathan. Mom and Jonathan knew each other well, as I always invited him to my family gatherings when I came up to visit. She gave me a hug and a kiss, then walked over to my grandmother and embraced her. I noticed that she and Sara only exchanged a curt nod. She then walked up to my father's chest and bowed her head. After a moment, she made the sign of the cross and walked away. When she came back over, she hugged Raquel, and I noticed her eyes were swollen and red.

"Are you okay, Mami?" I asked, putting my hands on her shoulders.

"Yes . . . Just a lot of memories." She sniffled.

"I'm surprised you came," I said.

"I came for you."

I smiled gently.

"It's not fun to go back, but it was thirty years ago. I've made my peace with it."

I thanked Jonathan for coming. "It means so much that you always show up for me," I said while giving his hand a squeeze.

"You're family, Em," he smiled. "Besides, you're about to repay the favor."

"Why is that?" I asked.

"Daniela and I set a date."

"No way!" I exclaimed, a little too loud. "It's about time. Congratulations!"

Daniela and Jonathan had been together five years and were a great fit, so I was elated that he was ready to commit. He told me to expect an email with more details, and then he left.

When the service concluded, we took our urns, and my grandmother and Sara agreed to stop by the house the next day. Raquel and I grabbed some pizza on our way home and ate lunch while watching Law & Order reruns the rest of the day.

We both fell asleep on the couch.

My grandmother stopped by the next morning to collect some of my father's personal items. While they were in Raquel's bedroom, I peered out the kitchen window. Sara was sitting in the car, staring blankly ahead. Remembering that no one really spoke to her the day before, I decided to swallow my pride and go outside.

She saw me approach the car and rolled her eyes before slipping her sunglasses on. I walked over to the driver's side and tapped on her window. She visibly sighed before rolling it down.

"What's up?" she asked, still staring ahead.

"We didn't speak yesterday," I said.

"You said plenty the day before."

"I want to apologize for my attitude. Tensions were high, and I was tired."

She nodded, then looked down at her lap.

I would have liked to hear an apology from her as well, but I knew it wouldn't happen.

"One more thing."

"Yes?" she asked, turning to look at me.

"I know you're angry. It's clear that you didn't want to come. Neither did I. My father did not deserve the fanfare. He never has. I want you to know that I understand your frustration at having to console your mother over the one kid that *never* appreciated her. I also know that just because you were never close to him, doesn't mean you aren't mourning. You mourn for the brother you never got to have."

She stared at me through her glasses, her lips quivering, and tears streaming down her face. She nodded, unable to speak.

Just then, my grandmother and Raquel walked out. Sara quickly wiped her tears, and we all exchanged our farewells.

3

SAGE ADVICE

"How was your week, Nathan?" Ann asked.

His session had begun thirty minutes ago. As always, he tried to kill time with small talk while he stared out the window.

Ann's office was in a business park with a large courtyard. There were trees planted throughout the yard with birdbaths and bird feeders that stood amid the flower gardens. The landscaping offered a serene view in the spring. Now in November, the birds were gone, and the small trees turned a deep crimson—their leaves slowly falling to their death.

He knew that feeling all too well.

"Uneventful," Nate said, still looking out the window.

"I see. Last week you mentioned you were taking an extended leave from work. Did you get that finalized?"

"Yes, it began this past week. I'll be off for a few months, but I don't think I'll return."

"Why do you say that?"

Nate could tell by Ann's posture and intense gaze that she

suspected he was speaking metaphorically. She had helped him through a suicidal episode before and was trying to discern whether he was in that head space again.

"I mean that literally, Ann," he reassured her. "I'm also considering a change of scenery."

She relaxed back into her chair.

Nate began seeing Ann shortly after receiving his first major promotion, when his anxiety had really taken off. They'd worked together on and off for over a decade. As with most of his academic endeavors, he put all his time and energy into mastering the role, quickly climbing the ladder to an executive position.

Trouble was, Nate hated his career. All of it.

The assholes he worked with and the corporate politics. All the personal sacrifices made for a dollar. He would have been long gone if it weren't for the comfortable lifestyle it afforded him and Emilia. She worked to keep herself busy, not out of necessity.

He had tried to build a decent life for her, as promised.

Brick by boring brick.

"You mentioned you are 'also' considering a change of scenery. Are you referring to Emilia? Have you spoken to her?"

"No. I haven't spoken to her since she walked out. I sent her a text last month sending my condolences for her father's passing, but I didn't receive a reply." Nate's words gritted against his teeth as he struggled to unclench his jaw.

"I sense anger in your tone . . . Can we talk about Emilia?" she asked.

Nate had resumed his weekly therapy sessions after Emilia left. The sessions helped him organize his thoughts and emotions, but he refused to discuss his wife. He was still too angry to listen to anyone rationalize her actions. After a month, however, she needed to be addressed.

"What do you want to talk about?" Nate challenged as he looked Ann in the eyes.

"How do you feel about Emilia leaving?"

He shrugged. "Worthless. My wife of twenty years, whom I've faithfully loved, told me she doesn't love me anymore, packed her car, and left the state. Even while I cried and begged her to stay, she stared back at me with a blank face. Like I didn't matter . . . My mother used to have that same fucking look on her face while watching my stepfather beat the shit out of me."

Ann studied him as he angrily swiped tears.

"I just want to understand what about me is not worth fighting for? How is it that the only women I've ever loved can just . . . toss me aside? I know I've struggled over the years and I'm not perfect, but I love my wife, and it hurts beyond belief that I'm not even afforded the opportunity to make this right."

"Make what right?"

"I don't know! It would be nice if she told me what I did wrong in the first place. I'd settle for her speaking to me at all . . ."

Ann paused while Nate regained his composure. He always appreciated her patience and serenity. It balanced the chaos he brought into the room.

"While we can't negate your experience in this situation, the truth is, we only have your vantage point. We can't understand Emilia's without hearing her side, so until that happens, maybe we can work to ensure that your vantage point isn't clouded by your pain. Who knows, maybe you hold the answer to some of these questions?"

He nodded while staring down at his class ring. He'd been

mindlessly spinning it around his finger. He was still angry, but she had a point.

Objectivity can only help matters, he thought.

"So, tell me more about your plans for the next few months."

His eyes fixed on the falling leaves again. "Some overdue soul searching, I guess."

I stared at the digital clock on the wooden dresser.

Four a.m.

I am usually a sound sleeper, but this past week, I'd been jolted awake at the same time every morning. The nightmares were so intense, I'd awakened to what I thought was a drum solo in my ears. It took a few moments to realize it was my heartbeat.

All this reminiscing about my father, dealing with Sara, and being in this new—or old—environment was clearly taking a toll. I would wake up to a drenched pillow and feel exhausted, my body aching from head to toe. After stretching my neck and hips, I made my way to the restroom.

My reflection was ghastly.

My eyes were puffy and red from crying in my sleep again. For a moment, I regretted my decision to leave North Carolina. Maybe coming up here wasn't going to work out the way I had intended.

After my father's funeral, I settled into Raquel's guest room and ironed out my next steps. I would eventually look for a job, but I had a cushy nest egg, so I wasn't in a rush. My priority was to settle into my own space, then find work nearby. As much as Raquel and I loved each other, we have always valued our independence. One day while I was straightening her hair, I made her aware of my apartment search.

"Emi, you don't have to go. That room is vacant, and I can move the supplies into my bedroom."

"No, Flaca. I need to anchor down somewhere, and I don't want to impose on your space. Besides, I'd like to live somewhere new, preferably on the North Shore."

"Well, there's no rush. You are welcome to stay as long as you need."

I pulled her head up toward me. "Thank you," I said as I kissed her forehead.

Apartment hunting in the suburbs is vastly different from a large city. While I found a few complexes I liked, most listings were in residential homes. After touring a few properties, I realized I didn't want to lock myself into a lease in case I didn't like the area. Instead, I searched for monthly rentals on Airbnb.

There were several homes that had private spaces for rent, so I messaged the homeowners to schedule a tour before booking online. Having lined up a few tours later that morning, I figured I might as well start my day.

As I headed to the kitchen, I was so focused on firing up the tea kettle, I didn't notice Raquel already sitting at the table until her chair creaked.

I let out a scream that could rival a banshee.

"Jeez, Emi! Wake up the block, why don't you?" Raquel laughed and she sipped out of her mug.

"Do you always sit in your kitchen in the middle of the night with all the lights off?"

"Not always, but I do from time to time. I use this time to reflect."

"You wake up at four in the morning to reflect? No way. You're having trouble sleeping again, aren't you?"

"Yes," she admitted. "Dad has been visiting regularly, and it's starting to creep me out."

"What do you mean?"

"I've been dreaming of him every night since he passed. Usually it's just flashbacks, childhood memories. He looks so handsome, and he's got a bright smile, but when he speaks, I can't hear anything. He talks, but there's no sound. It's like he's muted."

"That is weird," I said as I poured water over my tea bag.

"You don't dream of him, Emi?"

"Nope." *Now, that is a lie.*

I sat across from her and sipped my tea while she mindlessly twirled at a piece of her hair.

"I'm going to see a few Airbnb rentals today, do you want to go with me?"

"Can't. I am volunteering at the animal shelter."

"You love animals so much, why don't you have a pet?"

"My mom didn't like animals, and I promised myself I would get one after she passed, but I could never choose which one to bring home. For now, I just love on them until they get adopted."

"And if they don't?"

"We have an amazing outreach team, so there is quick turnover."

"Well, that's good."

"Emi are you sure you want to go?"

She had a focused expression, as if trying to mentally persuade me to change my mind.

"Yes, Flaca. Its time."

She sighed.

I broke the tension by asking about her love life,
and as I expected, she had some entertaining stories for me.
We laughed until the sun rose.

It took a miracle to look halfway decent. My eyes looked so tired, and my hair was not cooperating, but I managed to slick it back into a bun and tried a dewy makeup look to mask the sleep deprivation.

I would be driving in opposite directions to tour the homes, so I decided I would stop at my favorite bodega for lunch.

The first home was *very* nice. It was a split ranch with a converted garage. The older gentleman was so sweet. He informed me that the space used to be his man cave, but he decided to list it to supplement his retirement income.

As soon as I stepped inside, it was an immediate no.

It reeked of cigarette smoke, and I struggled to control my gag reflex as he spoke. This violent reaction was surprising, as I had grown up around a smoker. Only a few minutes had passed, but I felt like I was going to be sick and hastily made my exit.

As soon as I got in my car, I took off my sweater and stuffed it in a bag. I pulled an aromatherapy roller out of my purse and rubbed the oil under my nostrils. I welcomed the spicy peppermint scent and tried to take several deep breaths. My heartbeat began to slow.

I had known something was amiss for a while now, but I could never figure out why. The panic attacks were now frequent and seemed to be set off by the most random events. I rolled down the windows and headed to the next showing. The crisp autumn air had me feeling normal by the time I arrived.

The next house deserved its own catfish episode.

It was a small, one-story home that was barely visible behind overgrown shrubs. There was nowhere to park because of the rundown boat blocking the driveway. I suspected the pictures listed on Airbnb were from when the house was first built.

I messaged the host feigning illness, then kept driving.

Since I had a couple of hours before the next showing, I decided to stop for lunch early.

The bodega looked exactly as I remembered it. The owner, now much older, was chopping away at some chicken while an assembly line formed to help him to prepare their famous sandwiches. The overwhelming smell of fresh-baked Cuban bread filled my senses.

I ordered the usual—a chicken sandwich with noodle soup—then waited in my car. Even though everyone inside seemed friendly, I always had this weird feeling that I wasn't welcome. As I ate in my car, I stared out into the main street. The years may pass, but this town has not changed a bit.

I hated growing up here, and yet I looked around longingly.

There were so many painful experiences, but there were also wonderful memories, like when Nate and I would walk to this very bodega after school and split a chicken sandwich. I realized I had lost track of time when my phone alerted me it was time to leave. I hopped back on the highway and said a quick prayer that this showing would not be a complete waste of time.

As I drove past the affluent neighborhoods, I reminisced about the day trips I had taken with my mom as a child. On the rare occasions she had a day off, we would ride through these neighborhoods for hours, Mom always staring at these homes with such yearning.

"Algun dia, si Dios quiere," she would mutter to herself, *someday, God willing.* The type of poverty found in her homeland does not exist here. Just the opportunity to have a home to call her own was her American dream.

The place I was touring next was in a port town. When I approached my destination, my hope surged. It was a beautiful, high ranch with white siding and tall bay windows. The front lawn was landscaped with fall flowers and neatly trimmed shrubs. Pumpkins on haystacks lined the steps leading up to the front door and a harvest wreath hung above the door knocker.

Before I had a chance to knock, the door swung open, and a woman appeared.

Time stopped as I took her in.

She was about five-foot-six and had the most beautiful salt and pepper mane I'd had ever seen. Her long waves looked freshly tousled, and her bangs framed her face perfectly. What shocked me were her large, almond-shaped eyes. I'd never seen an icy shade of green like that before, and I was mesmerized. Her olive skin glowed as if she'd just walked off the beach, and her full lips were lightly glossed. She was dressed in a white, square-neck shirt tucked into soft, wide-leg pants.

It was so much to take in, I didn't notice when she approached me and wrapped me in her arms.

Her scent! It was soft and sensual, like roses dipped in a vanilla cream and wrapped in cashmere.

"Emilia! ¡Mucho gusto, mi amor! Come in, come in! It's getting nippy outside."

"Thank you for having me," I whispered, still entranced by her beauty.

The surprises just kept mounting.

I followed her up the half staircase to the living room, which could have qualified as a plant sanctuary. The main wall held a collage of perky plants on wooden shelves, and sconces hung with fresh herbs and flowers. A large bay window fully illuminated the space which screamed *come in and rest!*

There was a large loveseat adorned with throws and colorful pillows, a round mauve shag rug, and small candles lit throughout the room. Oddly, there was no TV. Instead, there was a large wood-burning fireplace and a built-in bookcase full to the brim with well-worn books.

"Welcome to your new home!" she exclaimed with a confidence that disarmed me.

As I emerged from my fandom, I managed to say, "I'm sorry I didn't catch your name on the listing, I just saw Sage on your profile."

"That is my name. My mother named me Salvia—Sage in English—because my eyes were this color straight out of the womb!"

YES! That's it. Her eyes were a vibrant sage green!

"It is very fitting."

"I think so too!" she laughed.

God, even that was intoxicating.

"Would you like some tea?"

"Yes, that would be great."

She pulled a smoked glass pitcher out of the fridge and poured me a cup of iced tea.

"Now let me give you a tour."

From the outside, the house blended in with all the others on the street, but the interior was plucked out of a design magazine. The kitchen had beautiful, off-white cabinets with brass handles, a large island with a butcher block countertop, and a built-in gas range. The other appliances were obviously top of the line, and there was a classic black-and-white tile floor. At the end, there were French doors leading out to a large deck. To the right, there was a hallway.

"The guest bathroom is this door on the right, and my bedroom is at the end," she said, pointing to double doors at the end of the hall.

"Your home is stunning, Sage," I mused.

"I'm glad you like it. But we haven't gotten to the best part!"

She excitedly led me back to the entrance area, then down the half stairs to the lower level. As Sage slid open the pocket doors, I took in the massive study on the left. A large, tidy, modern desk stood in the middle, and the entire back wall was made of built-in, floor-to-ceiling bookcases, again stacked with books. There was even a librarian's ladder to reach the top.

"My goodness, this office is out of a magazine!"

"Thank you. As you can tell, I love to read," she giggled.

Her library included all sorts of genres; herbology, indigenous culture, politics, economics, romance, and poetry.

"Emilia?"

"Hmm?" I was so engrossed with the study I didn't hear her walk over to the other room.

When I spun around my jaw dropped. This was *not* the room in the listing.

"Sage? This is not the room in the listing."

"Of course, it is," she said, perplexed.

I pulled out my phone and showed her the listing we had chatted about, and her eyes widened.

She burst into laughter and the beautiful sound echoed in the room.

This woman could not be real! She was so vibrant it was unnerving.

"My apologies, I must have uploaded the wrong photos to the site. I'm not tech savvy. Those pictures are for another listing. I just renovated a home a few blocks away."

I tried to hide my disappointment. The pictures were nice, but nowhere as beautiful as this home.

"Regardless, this suite is available, and to make up for the inconvenience, I will lease it for the same price."

"Really?" I could not mask my excitement.

"Yes, absolutely!"

"How long can I stay?" I asked, a little too eagerly.

"The first booking is two weeks. If we are a good fit, you can re-book up to ninety days," she explained, her smile warm and comforting.

"I'll take it!"

As I finished the tea, which Sage told me was made of chamomile, lemongrass, and stevia leaf, all sourced from her indoor garden, she gave me a lot of great resources about the town, places to eat, and what parks to visit.

As I got ready to leave, she gave me the warmest hug; it nearly brought tears to my eyes. I didn't realize I'd been so starved for affection.

"Emilia, I'm so excited we found each other."

"Me too, Sage. Thanks again," I said, as I got in my car and drove away.

For the first time in years, I felt like I had made a friend.

———————

I stopped at the grocery store on my way back to Raquel's place to pick up ingredients for beef burgundy. I wanted to make her dinner for a change, and I figured it was a pleasant way to break the news about my departure. Besides, the domestic tasks always allowed me to process my thoughts, and I hadn't cooked a meal since I had left North Carolina.

Since I left Nate . . .

The twinge in my gut returned. It had been a month since I last spoke to him, and I found myself worrying about his state of mind. I knew he was still alive, because I received a phone notification whenever he armed and disarmed the alarm system. But whether he was taking his anti-depressants, going to therapy, or even eating properly, I didn't know. Nate was never the best cook. I hoped he wasn't living off sandwiches.

As I washed and chopped the mushrooms, carrots, and garlic, I tried to pinpoint what it was about Sage that made her so hypnotic. After I seared the chuck roast, I deglazed the Dutch oven with fresh beef stock, then added my vegetables, pearl onions, some thyme and bay leaves, and a splash of Pinot Noir.

Raquel walked in as I placed the pot in the oven. "What is that smell?" she said as she closed her eyes and breathed in.

"Beef Bourguignon," I said as I took a sip of my Pinot.

"Beef burgernon? I've never heard of it," she repeated with a funny expression.

I laughed so hard, I had to spit my wine into the kitchen sink.

"What?" she asked, giggling as she poured herself a glass.

"Yes, Flaca. Beef burgernon. That's tonight's dinner."

A couple of hours later, we were sitting on her back patio eating while I relayed the day's events.

"I need to meet this woman, she sounds amazing."

"She is . . . I decided to book the room on a month-to-month basis," I said hesitantly.

"Booo."

"I'll still come visit, Sis."

"It's okay, Emi. I understand. Besides, I won't be alone. I took your advice and decided to adopt a kitten." She pulled out her phone and showed me pictures of a tiny male kitten she named Gomez. "He's still not weaned, but once he's ready, he's coming home with me."

"That's excellent news! I can't wait to meet the little guy."

"Oh, I forgot to mention . . . this came in the mail for you." She reached into her purse and pulled out a tan envelope.

It had a North Carolina postmark.

4

SWEET DREAMS (OF YOU)

The nightmare always begins at this moment.

Raquel and I are asleep on the couch.

Suddenly, I am shaken awake and Marta whispers in my ear, "When your dad comes inside, stay quiet, and do not let her cry."

The pounding on the door intensifies. I turn to face Raquel who is lightly snoring. My heart is beating so fast, it feels like it's humming. He breaks through the door and stumbles into the living room shouting Marta's name.

"You fucking idiot! Where did you put them!" His words are slurred. When he gets drunk, he shouts for hours.

Sometimes he does worse . . .

On a good night, we all just nod along while he hurls insults at everyone. Tonight, is not a good night.

Dad wants the car, and Marta can't allow that. She needs to go to work in the morning, and I'm going back to my mom's house in just a couple weeks, so we have to buy school supplies. She can't afford another car or bail again. They can't even afford their own place, so I sleep on the couch at Grandma's house while everyone else sleeps in the guest room. If Marta can convince him to go to bed, we are clear; he may just pass out.

As soon as Marta walks into the living room, however, he rushes towards her. I hear his fist crack against her jaw, and then howls of pain as he drags her to their bedroom by the hair.

"Don't EVER take the goddamn car again!" he roars as he continues to punch her.

I hold my hands to Raquel's ears, so she doesn't wake up. If he hears her cry, he'll come back out. She may only be three years old, but even that won't save her.

There is furniture crashing and more yelling. Marta hid the keys well this time.

Grandma comes out of her room to plead with him. "Pablo, please stop. You promised you wouldn't beat on her anymore. Go to bed, and you can take the car in the morning, okay?"

"If you know what's good for you, you'll go back to bed." His menacing tone is no bluff.

Grandma retreats to her bedroom.

He staggers back into the living room and continues his search.

My heartbeat is now in sync with his footsteps. It stops whenever he does.

I can feel him hovering over us now, and his hand brushes against my shoulder. I try my best not to tense up at his touch. He lightly shoves me out of the way, then Raquel, to make sure we aren't hiding them.

He finally gives up and throws himself on the recliner. A few minutes later, I hear his snores. After a few moments, Marta tiptoes into the living room and gently removes his work boots.

She then heads to the kitchen to grab an ice pack. She collapses on the other couch and quietly sobs for what seems like hours.

Then, silence. A deafening silence . . .

Once I've lost all sensation, I fall asleep.

Nate had just finished putting his groceries away when he heard paws at the kitchen door, followed by the sweetest meow.

He chuckled as he emptied cat food into a bowl. "I'm coming, little one."

A couple weeks ago, Ann suggested he try therapeutic letter writing to promote better internal dialogue. He poured himself a hefty glass of Stagg and headed to the back patio, pen and paper in hand. After an hour, he hadn't written a single word, but had a healthy dose of Bourbon coursing through his veins.

Nate was beginning to drift off when he had heard rustling behind one of the neatly trimmed hedges. His curiosity piqued, he went to investigate and found a tuxedo cat with a bright pink nose lounging behind the bush. On her flank, was a friendly kitten that sauntered up to his leg and nuzzled him.

The mother cat was also surprisingly social, and against his better judgment, he went inside to grab some leftover steak to feed them. That routine continued until a week ago when the kitten returned alone.

While at the store, he decided to grab cat food and a cardboard house. As soon as he placed the bowl on the ground, the kitten began to chow down, growling with every bite.

"Slow down, food's not going anywhere." Nate smiled as he stroked her back while she devoured her meal.

He'd given a lot of thought to what Ann had said. He kept rehashing old memories, looking for holes in his vantage point.

Emilia's last pregnancy and subsequent miscarriage had taken an enormous toll on their relationship. She had been farther along than the two previous times and believed she could carry to term. Only when she had cleared her twelve-week checkup did she entertain picking out a name.

"If it's a boy, I think he should be a Junior," she said as she laid her head on his lap.

"I can get down with that. And if it's a girl?"

She paused for a second, then giggled. "What do you think of . . . Capri?"

"Capri?" he asked, perplexed. "Like . . . a Capri Sun?"

"No! Like the song by Colbie Caillat." She looked up and noticed his confused expression. Emilia hopped off the bed and grabbed her iPod from the dresser.

She handed him an earbud and pressed play. The song was about a mother expecting a baby girl named Capri. It had a sweet acoustic melody that had made quite the impression on Emilia.

In that moment, Nate was reminded why he had fallen in love with her. She had the most beautiful smile. Warmth radiated from her when she was happy.

When she was hopeful.

A couple weeks later, Emilia suffered a late miscarriage which required a surgical procedure. He hadn't seen her smile like that since.

One day, as he cleaned the house, he spotted her iPod in the trash along with the torn ultrasound pictures. She had previously destroyed evidence of her last two pregnancies, and normally, he didn't protest, but this time felt different.

This time, they had picked out a name . . .

He took the shreds out of the waste bin and put them in his pocket. He found her in their closet sitting cross-legged and reorganizing shoes.

"Honey, are you okay? Shouldn't you be in bed?" he asked.

"I'm fine." She didn't look up. Her voice sounded hollow.

Nate's eyes welled with tears. He felt so helpless when he saw her like that.

She noticed his expression and sighed, "Oh, please, Nate. Don't start with the tears again." Another typical response; downplaying traumatic situations.

"Em, I'm worried about you, and I'm sad about our baby. I don't mean to be emotional but—"

"What are you emotional about, Nathan? Did you have to lay on the bathroom floor in a pool of blood again? On top of losing my baby, I have to deal with that disappointed look on your face. Well, I'm sorry. I don't know what to say. Motherhood is just a sick game the universe insists on playing with me."

"I'm not disappointed in you, Baby. I'm worried about you. You've shut down again. That can't be healthy."

Emilia snapped, "Spare me the mental health speech, Nate. Just because you need therapy, doesn't mean I do too."

The low blows were becoming a habit. Not wanting to argue, Nate left the room. Emilia was in distress, but that didn't excuse her harsh words. They reminded him of his childhood when he would attempt to console his mom after a beating, and she would dismiss him, or worse, *ridicule* him for being "dramatic."

In retrospect, he could have been more understanding with both of them. Instead, he chose to withdraw, and decided not to ask her how she was feeling anymore.

Nate had never considered owning a pet with his busy schedule, but the kitten was just too cute to leave outside. He picked her up and she immediately nuzzled into his neck.

He sighed, "Come on, Capri, we're going to the vet."

———

The pet clinic was unusually busy for a weeknight. Post-pandemic protocol required that he wait in the car until his buzzer went off.

With Capri napping in the passenger seat, he decided he would write his first letter to Emilia. He wasn't sure what had possessed him to suggest written correspondence.

Desperation, perhaps . . .

He kept it short and sweet. Nate hoped she would at least consider having a conversation. He sealed the envelope when his cellphone rang.

It was Jonathan.

He hesitated. Nate hadn't spoken to his brother in several years. Their last phone conversation had not gone well, and he decided it was best that Jonathan remain in the past. That is, until last month when Jonathan had texted him with news about Emilia's father.

What if something had happened to Emilia?

He answered, "Hey, Jon."

"Nate?"

"That's who you called."

"Yeah, I . . . I just didn't expect you to answer . . ."

"It's your lucky day. Everything okay?"

"Yeah. Everything's cool . . . how are you doing?"

"I'm doing alright . . . Have you heard from Emilia? Is she okay?"

"Yeah, she's doing well. When I last spoke to her, she mentioned that she found an Airbnb on the North Shore and is moving in this week."

Nate's heart sank. He'd really hoped she would return. What if she was truly ready to move on?

"I see."

"Nate, the reason for my call . . . I proposed to Daniela."

"Wow! Congratulations. You've been with her for a while now."

"Thanks! She's my best friend."

That stung.

There had been a time when Jonathan and Nathan were best friends, navigating the war zone that was their home.

"I'm happy for you bud."

"Nathan, I want you to be my best man."

Silence.

Excitement and dread rushed to the surface at once.

"Nate?"

"Yeah."

"Did you hear me?"

Reigning in his emotion, he replied, "Let me know when and where. I'll be there."

Jonathan's sigh of relief was palpable.

"Question," Nate said, "will Emilia be there?"

"Yeah, she's invited."

"Okay. Don't tell her I'm coming, okay?

"Okay . . ."

"One more thing . . . Do you have Raquel's address?"

I had just finished bringing in the last of my belongings, when Sage entered the room holding a tray.

"Here is some fresh tea and a sandwich!" she declared as she placed it on the corner desk.

"That looks lovely! You really didn't have to . . ."

"It's my pleasure! Let me know if you need anything, I'll be on my deck reading."

"Oh, what are you reading?"

"A mystery novel about a couple who disappeared and a psychologist that suspects their children had something to do with it. I can't wait to finish!"

"Let me know how it ends."

"Will do," Sage said as she left.

I surveyed my new home. The guest suite was spectacular.

And *massive*.

Slightly larger than my master suite in North Carolina, it had ten-foot walls painted a soft, pale green. Tall French doors led out to the patio, and two egg chairs hung under Sage's upper deck.

There was a large, California king bed on an upholstered bedframe which complimented the abstract accent rug and chic accessories, and two long windows on either side of the bed that allowed for plenty of natural light. There was even a kitchenette with an impressive coffee bar that included a Nespresso machine and mini fridge. In the corner stood a small writers' desk where Sage had placed a fresh flower bouquet and welcome binder. A white fabric chandelier tied the room design together.

If I wasn't already impressed, the bathroom sealed the deal. The walls were tiled from floor to ceiling in my favorite color, teal.

The fixtures were brass, and a deep white claw-footed tub stood next to a double rain shower.

It wasn't just pretty. It felt like an oasis.

From the moment I had stepped into the space, I felt all the tension I'd been carrying in the last month begin to dissipate.

After putting my clothes away in the dresser and storing my belongings in the closet, I took a long, warm shower.

It was only eleven a.m., but after another restless night, I decided to take a nap.

I awoke to a delicious aroma. It smelled like my mom's cooking.

As my eyes adjusted, I realized it was dark outside. I peered over at the alarm clock on the bedside table.

Five p.m.

Not only had I slept like a rock for six hours, I hadn't had a single nightmare.

It was remarkable how well rested I felt, so I hopped to my feet, freshened up, and threw on some warm clothes. I was looking forward to exploring the town at sundown.

As I climbed the stairs to the front entrance, Sage called out to me.

"Emilia! Dinner is ready!"

I stopped in my tracks, dumbfounded. Once I processed what she said, I slowly walked up the steps to the main floor. "You made me dinner, Sage?"

"Yes, Honey! Remember? I told you I was making you a welcome dinner tonight."

"No ..." I'd been so tired lately, I probably zoned out when she told me.

"I'm sorry, I mentioned it while you were pulling items out of your trunk ... I should have confirmed. If you made other plans, I understand."

"No! it's fine. I'd love to stay for dinner, and I'm flattered that you thought of me."

She flashed her radiant smile.

I sat in the dining room while Sage brought our plates to the table. She had prepared a Caribbean style arroz con pollo topped with avocado and paired it with mixed greens and a passionfruit dressing.

"¡Buen Provecho!"

"¡Gracias!" I smiled.

Then, I took my first bite and almost cried. "My GOD, Sage. This tastes so good. I'll have to get your recipe."

"The next time I make it, you can watch me. I don't follow a recipe; I just add a little bit of what feels right in the moment."

I chuckled and proceeded to pace my bites. It took a conscious effort. Had I been alone, I would have inhaled my plate.

"I can't quite place your accent, but it doesn't sound native to New York?"

"No, I moved to NYC from LA about ten years ago for work. Eventually I grew tired of the city life and settled here in the suburbs. Your accent is hard to peg as well."

"Yeah, I was born and raised here on Long Island, but we moved to North Carolina when I was twenty. My accent has neutralized over the years."

"Ah, so your family is still in North Carolina?"

"No . . . my husband is. We separated, and I came back up

North to reset." I paused, expecting more questions, but she continued.

"I know the feeling," she said as she began to clear our plates, "I also relocated in hopes of a fresh start."

"May I ask what you do for work?" I followed her back into the kitchen.

"I've flipped several real estate properties in town. Some are Airbnbs, some long-term rentals."

She handed me a towel, and we cleaned dishes together.

Time slowed down in this place. There were no racing thoughts, no problems to solve. Just two people enjoying the mundane. It was *lovely*.

Sage grabbed dessert out of the fridge, a flan she had made earlier that day, and invited me out to her deck for dessert. She lit an exquisite glass firepit and its warmth instantly cut through the November chill. Coupled with the string lights hanging from the glass balcony, it felt like we were lounging at a rooftop bar.

Sage was such a disarming figure. I found myself sharing personal stories about my marriage, my infertility issues, and the events that led up to my move.

"And you don't picture Nathan in your future, Emilia?"

"Not the Nathan I left behind, no. He wants to work on things, but . . . how do you make someone *want* to show you attention? Affection?"

"You can't," she conceded.

"I have felt so lost, for so long. I want to learn how to feel again."

"Feel what?"

Anything . . .

When I didn't respond, she added "I spent a great deal of time seeking happiness."

"You've clearly achieved that," I said while gesturing around me.

"This? This is just a manifestation of battles hard fought. My battles were internal. There was a time when chaos ruled my heart and mind, and it manifested externally. When I began to heal, the world around me changed."

"When you say battles . . ."

"There were many, Emilia. Anger, bitterness, resentment, self-sabotage. Ultimately, they all tied back to my greatest foe, unforgiveness."

I swallowed.

She continued. "Unforgiveness acts like an infarction to the heart . . . a slow festering of bitterness, slowly eating away at your happiness, leaving only stench and decay in its place. It is a slow death. Tragically, we don't even recognize it until it has consumed us."

What an awful way to live, I thought. Sure, there were difficult memories, but I wasn't one to hold a grudge. The past is just that . . .

Her other "battles," however, resonated with me.

Sage shared stories of her turbulent childhood, which sounded a lot like mine. Her parents immigrated to the US in the seventies, and she spent her early years with her grandparents.

That was the happiest she'd ever been.

When Sage's mother sent for her, her carefree childhood vanished. If she wasn't in school, cooking, or doing chores, she was helping her mom clean houses. Her father was a womanizer who could never hold down a job.

"I wish I could say those were the worst of my troubles, Emilia . . . My father's brother moved in with us when I was twelve years old." She stared out into the backyard. "He became the villain in my story."

She met my concerned expression with a soft smile.

Overwhelmed by such heavy topics, we decided to call it a night.

After we cleaned up, I insisted that I would take her out to lunch the next day. She agreed on the condition that she would show me around town.

Once I was back in my room, I threw on my pajamas and climbed into bed. The linens were incredibly soft, and the pillows were just right. I was relaxed and felt my body melt into the bed, but I just could not fall asleep.

After a moment, I realized what I'd forgotten. I pulled the envelope out of my purse and opened Nate's letter.

Em,

I've never actually written a letter before, so please forgive if my inexperience shows . . . I just wanted to say that I miss you . . . so much.

I miss how the scent of your perfume lingers in the bathroom.

I miss seeing your favorite slippers in the foyer.

I miss hearing your laughter while you watch The Office reruns.

I know I did a bad job of showing you that. And for that, I am sorry.

That aside, I am surviving here on my own. After four weeks, I got sick of eating sandwiches, so I signed up for a cooking class.

I'm back in therapy and think I'm making progress. I've also joined a gym and the physical activity greatly helps my mood.

How are you doing? I hope you are at peace and surrounded by people that love you. If you ever want to talk, say the word and I'll give you a ring.

Love you always,
Nate

I put the letter back in my purse and shut off the bedside lamp.

Then, I let the tears take me.

5

THANKS FOR THE MEMORIES

June 2002

"By The Way" by Red Hot Chili Peppers was blasting on the radio when I took the phone off its speaker.

"Okay, I really have to go now, my mom is going to be home soon, and I'm almost done."

"But," Nate protested, "then I'll miss your voice and lay around waiting for you to call again . . ."

"No, you won't. You'll go play ball with Jonathan, help your mom around the house, and hide the breakables."

He chuckled. "It's kind of weird that you already know my routine so well."

"No, it's not . . . it's basically my own," I muttered as I swept up the broken glass from last night. I heard the familiar sound of my mom's car rolling into the driveway. "Gotta go, Babe."

"Bye, Beautiful," he said before the phone clicked.

I started the dishwasher and was switching laundry loads when my mom walked in. I had planned to clean a little more, even get her laundry started so she could get some rest, but she was home early. She'd been up all night, fighting with her boyfriend. After throwing his belongings out on the front lawn, she had retreated to her bedroom and cried until the sun rose.

On my way home, I had stopped by 7Eleven to grab some frozen pizzas so she wouldn't have to cook.

She murmured a faint greeting as she walked past me, and I could tell she was exhausted. Her hazel eyes were swollen and her face flushed.

As soon as she got to the sink, I heard a loud sigh. She slammed her lunchbox on the counter.

"Emilia, come here!" she shouted.

I rolled my eyes as I turned around and headed for the kitchen.

What did I do this time? "Yeah?" I answered.

"Why is it so hard for you keep this kitchen clean?"

I looked around at the kitchen I had just spent an hour deep cleaning, annoyance radiating out of me. "It *is* clean," I gritted.

Before I could tell her about the chores I'd done, she grabbed a metal spoon I had left in the sink and hurled it at me, hitting me square in the chest.

"Ow! What the hell is your problem?" I shouted, trying my best not to cry. That shit hurt.

That's all it took.

Before I knew it, she was in my face, grabbing a fist full of my hair. "¡Mira, Pendeja!" she scathed. Her grip tightened around my hair, and I could feel tears pricking at the sides of my eyes. "I am sick and tired of your mouth. Let me remind you that I am your mother, and you *will* respect me!"

I was taller and stronger than her, but if I put up a fight, she'd grab something to hit me. Lately, our tussles were growing in intensity, and the bruises were getting harder to hide.

"I work two jobs, clean this house, cook every night, and keep you comfortable! Why can't your ungrateful ass keep a sink clean?"

I didn't respond. There was no point.

When she let go of me, I brushed past her to my room.

"Where is the meat I told you to take out of the freezer?" she yelled behind me.

I didn't answer and slammed my bedroom door so hard the hinges rattled. She hurried past my room to her own.

She'd be back with a belt.

Sage had stocked the mini fridge with sparkling water, fresh fruit, and a variety of creamers. The aroma of pumpkin and espresso had me salivating, and I couldn't wait to get outside. After weeks of sleepless nights, watching the sunrise had become a daily ritual.

It felt like I was getting a personalized greeting from the universe.

Coffee mug in hand, I threw on my fuzzy sherpa robe and headed out to the patio just as the sky turned a deep lavender. Dido's *Life for Rent* album played quietly on my phone while I admired Sage's manicured yard.

As I swung on a plush egg chair, I recalled Nate's letter. His sweet words filled me with so many emotions, mostly confusion and anger. I wanted to yell at him; to tell him that he doesn't get to play with my emotions in the eleventh hour.

I also wanted him to hold me . . . to feel safe like I had when we were young.

Eventually, the sun came out to greet me. Through the backyard trees, I saw bright orange rays blast through the sky, sending hues of pink, purple, and blue in every direction—every autumn leaf illuminated, as if they were light bulbs on a tree lamp.

It was a magical view. Just then, *See the Sun* began to play, which made me smile. The lyrics were fitting.

and I promise you, you'll see the sun again . . .

I knew then I was on the right path. I closed my eyes and could feel my smile widening.

After sending Raquel a quick text to invite her to lunch with me and Sage, I browsed through my closet for an outfit. Unsurprisingly, she responded right away. That insomnia of hers was still going strong. I promised to text her a time and place later in the day. My outfit of choice was a black knit sweater tucked into a plaid mini skirt, and I paired it with black leggings and a pair of Docs. I also made a mental note to purchase warmer clothing; winters in New York were far more severe than down south.

My hair now reached my shoulders, and I'd made the decision to grow it out; I hadn't worn it this long since I became a hair stylist. I went for a smokey eye look with a nude pink lip. When I was done, I smiled into the mirror.

I felt . . . *pretty*. Something in the air sparkled.

I felt on edge, but in a good way.

As I grabbed my handbag, I spotted Sage out in her backyard tending to her garden. She wore long, knee-high, wedge boots with burgundy leggings and a long slitted poncho. Her thick hair looked fabulous in a high, tousled bun.

"Morning, Sage," I called as I stepped outside.

She was pruning some plants at one of her raised stands. "Good morning! How did you sleep?" she asked, her bright smile shining.

"Wonderful, I've been sleeping a lot better lately. What are you up to?"

"I'm pruning my rosemary and southernwood; Gotta move these into the greenhouse for the winter," she said, pointing to a small tarp house in the corner by the shed.

"This garden is impressive," I said, once again admiring the landscape. She had constructed a curved raised bed in the shape of a half circle. Hydroponic towers stood at both ends.

"Why, thank you! The earth gives you everything you need my dear. You take care of it, it takes care of you."

It was clear that this was Sage's happy place. There was glow about her when she tended to her plants. She picked up the foliage and tossed it into a compost bin.

"What do you like to do for fun?" she asked.

I blushed, preparing my lame response. "I used to watch a lot of reality TV. I worked long hours at the salon, so I didn't really have energy for much outside of work."

"Nothing wrong with a little escapism. Besides, today is a new day. Another opportunity to discover a new interest."

"I look forward to that. I've been meaning to ask; may I check out a book from your library?"

She flashed her megawatt smile. "Go for it! Books are like my television; I can't get enough."

I helped her wheel her herb cart into the greenhouse, then we headed into town. Another point in Sage's favor was her taste in music. She, like me, loved a little bit of everything, as long as it had soul. We jammed to Queen, AC/DC, Billie Holiday, Marc

Anthony, and The Fugees, all by the time we made it to our first stop.

We arrived at her favorite local coffee shop and ordered vanilla lavender lattes and split a fresh bagel with veggie-flavored cream cheese.

Downtown was lively for a weekday. The sky was cloudless; a crisp blue backsplash for the sun to beam over the brightly colored shops. The bookstores, restaurants, and boutiques had their doors open to allow for ample airflow. Boats of various sizes were docked along the strip.

As we walked, Sage continued to share stories about her life. She was an only child and had decided not to have children of her own. She'd only been in one serious relationship before realizing that romantic love was not something she was interested in.

"I've found love in the world itself—nature, charity, arts and culture, and friendship—that fulfills me. And speaking of friendship, I will introduce you to a friend today. But first . . . " she pointed to a store across the street.

When we stepped into Emery's Bookstore, Sage's icy green eyes began to dance with excitement; she practically ran toward the new releases. I wandered over to the journal section, searching for a new notebook. I'd been trying to journal consistently for years, but the habit never stuck.

Just then my phone buzzed; Raquel confirmed what time she would meet us for lunch. I quickly replied, then looked up in time to spot Sage at the counter and ran toward her. Before she had a chance to reach for her wallet, I snatched the books out of her hand and handed them to the salesclerk.

"Absolutely not," she said, reaching for the books.

She may be taller, but I am quicker. "No, Ma'am," I asserted.

"Dinner, fruit, flowers, sandwiches, and then breakfast this morning; it's my turn."

I could tell she wanted to argue, but I was resolute, and she knew it. When she sighed, I flashed a victorious smile, then paid for our items.

Our last stop before lunch was a boutique called Fire Sign. It had a very eccentric feel. The vibe was electric and bright, like a simmering energy permeated throughout the store. There was a wide selection of handmade jewelry and clothing. An older woman stood at the register. She wore a long robe and multi-colored bangles on each wrist. Crystals and beads hung from her neck. The wrinkles on her face only accentuated her beauty; her years of laughter having left a physical trace. Gray locs sat atop her head in a high bun and her auburn glasses popped against her rich, sable skin.

"Andy," Sage squealed as they embraced. "I'd like you to meet my new friend, Emilia."

"Emilia! I'm Andrea, or Andy, very nice to meet you," she said as she took my hand.

"It's nice to meet you," I said as I looked around, my eyes catching the crystal laced dream catchers. "Is this your store?"

"Yes! Been here over ten years now."

"I love the name."

"Thank you! My sun, moon, and ascendant signs are all fire elements. I'm just a walking flamethrower," she said with a wink.

I nodded, assuming she was referring to her astrological signs.

Sage grabbed my arm. "Emilia is my guest for the foreseeable future, and I'm trying to get her acquainted with the village and its local gems. What spots do you reco—"

"Fire Sign," she shouted enthusiastically.

We burst into laughter.

"Oof, so many places," Andy said while she lazily rubbed her chin. "Emery's of course . . . there's Harry's poetry bar, Vana's yoga studio, Jewel's bagel shop, Vincenzo's, oh! And the Bluff. She would love the hidey spot."

"Oooh! The beaches were on our list, but you're right, she would *love* the hidey spot."

"The hidey spot?" I asked, tickled at the nickname.

Andy nodded, "There is a side entrance to the beach that people rarely use. Through the trees lies a small cove with a rocky shore. The water goes deep, so it's not really meant for swimming. Occasionally, you'll see a fisherman or two on the rocks. Otherwise, it is empty . . . Sage and I have spent countless evenings out there with our friends."

"Oh, just wait till we take you out there, Emilia! The stars are so bright at night," Sage mused.

While they discussed a new shipment Andy had received, I excused myself to look around the store. Most of the merchandise was handmade and sourced locally, although there was imported pottery and clothing from Central and South America.

I picked out a pair of earrings for Raquel, a crystal dreamcatcher, and a book on the Algonquian Peoples of Long Island. When I finally made my way back to the register, I noticed a man standing next to Andy and Sage.

His magnetism was . . . jarring.

When he spotted me, his smile grew, as if he recognized an old friend.

"Emilia, I'd like you to meet my son, William," Andy said.

"Call me Will, Emilia," he said as he extended his hand. His voice was gentle and his curious eyes glowed.

"Nice to meet you, Will," I replied, fighting the blush creeping up my neck.

"Emilia relocated from North Carolina and is staying with me for a while," Sage inserted with a knowing smirk.

Her matchmaking tone had me concerned . . .

"I see. Get tired of the south?" he asked.

"Something like that."

"Well, if you ever need a tour guide, I won't be as good as Sage —she knows everyone in this town—but I'd be happy to give it a shot.

"Thanks for the offer." I nodded.

The intensity in his gaze was alarming, but in a good way. I'd pay dollars for his thoughts . . .

"Okay, we have to get going." Sage gave Will and Andy a hug and kiss. "But I'll see you both at Friendsgiving, right?"

"We will be there," Will said, still looking at me.

I broke eye contact and followed Andy to the register.

"As much as I'd love to sell you this book, I'm pretty sure Sage already owns it," Andy said.

Just then, Sage peered over my shoulder. "Yep, I own it. You can borrow it."

I purchased the dream catcher and earrings, then Sage and I locked arms, and we walked down the block to the restaurant.

"What did you think of Will? Cute, huh?" she asked.

"He's handsome . . . "

"He's single, ya know. Almost got married last year, but things ended abruptly."

"Hmm."

"He's a wonderful guy." I could feel Sage's gaze on me. "You'll see."

I decided not to respond as we approached the restaurant. We were greeted by a pretty host, who appeared to be in her twenties. When she asked if we preferred indoor or outdoor seating, Sage all but shouted, "Outdoor!" then flashed her gorgeous smile. The hostess fell for her infectious charm and whisked us away to the deck.

The view was spectacular.

The restaurant overlooked the bay. Boats were docked nearby. In the distance we could see a small public beach where kids were playing.

We had just ordered drinks when Raquel entered the restaurant. I waved and she hurried over to us.

"Hey, Emi," she said as she gave me a kiss on the cheek.

"Flaca, I want you meet Sage."

Sage did not allow Raquel a chance to respond before engulfing her in a tight hug. Raquel's surprised expression was a Polaroid moment.

"Emi was right about you. You really are a ball of sunshine!"

"Emi? What a cute nickname," Sage said.

"Nate calls her Em. That's her husb—er, ex-husband . . . " Raquel glanced over at me nervously.

"It's okay, she knows about Nate," I reassured her.

"Like, all . . . about Nate?"

I chuckled. "She knows enough."

Sage and Raquel hit it off, naturally. Raquel is talkative, and Sage is *very* inquisitive. After Raquel divulged all the details of her jewelry making business, Sage promised to connect her with some of her contacts for networking opportunities.

I pulled out the turquoise earrings I had purchased at Fire Sign. "I got you a little gift, Flaca. I know you make jewelry, but I figured you'd like to wear something you haven't made, for a change."

"Oooh," she exclaimed as she studied the earrings, "I love them! I've always wanted to work with copper wire . . . This also happens to be Dad's favorite color."

My face fell, and I didn't have time to recover before Raquel and Sage noticed.

"Sorry," she quipped, then turned to face Sage. "Emilia hates our dad," she said matter-of-factly.

"I don't hate him," I declared, trying to reign in my defensiveness. "I don't particularly care for him, but I have never hated him."

She rolled her eyes. "Okay . . . she doesn't care for him. She stopped coming to visit in her teens, didn't tell him—or any of us —that she got married, and avoided him at all costs. But no, she doesn't hate him."

I had to pace my breathing. My face was flooded with embarrassment.

I don't know why she chose this moment to air her thoughts, but it was highly inappropriate. Sage may have chalked it up to Raquel being an open book. Her tone seemed flippant; she was even laughing it off.

I saw through all of it.

She had crossed the line. I would address it later, but this was not the time nor place. I noticed Sage studying my expressions and sensed there would be questions later. We ordered our food, and Sage changed subjects flawlessly. Pretty soon, we were all laughing hysterically while enjoying fresh seafood and mocktails.

As we wrapped up lunch, Sage asked, "Raquel, do you have plans next Wednesday?"

"No, I should be free . . ."

"Excellent! Emilia and I are hosting a Friendsgiving dinner."

"Oh, a party! I'd love to." Raquel smiled.

I had heard Friendsgiving mentioned back at Fire Sign but didn't realize Sage was hosting. I was even more surprised to hear I was hosting. My expression gave me away.

"Sorry, Emilia," Sage quickly added, "You don't have to do anything, you are an honorary host because you live with me."

"I'm just glad to be invited," I laughed.

I picked up the tab despite protests around the table. We bid our farewells, then headed back to the house.

On our way home, we stopped at the grocery store to grab a few household items.

"You are welcome to use the kitchen whenever you'd like, Emi,"Sage declared as she browsed the shopping aisle.

I found her use of my sister's nickname for me endearing. "Thank you. I prefer simple meals, but occasionally get the itch to cook a family style meal. I love making lasagna."

"Oh, lasagna sounds delicious!" Sage closed her eyes, as if remembering the last time she had some.

"Shall I whip some up for dinner tonight?" I asked, already looking for the pasta aisle.

"You must," she exclaimed.

As I picked out ingredients, Sage eyed the produce specials. "May I say something, at the risk of overstepping?" she asked behind me.

"Sure . . . " I said slowly.

"About Raquel's comments earlier . . . I understood your sentiments regarding your father. She perceives that you hate him, but family issues can be complex and gray. Sometimes, we have to love people, but from a distance."

I nodded. Another point in her favor—her uncanny ability to read me.

Sometimes better than myself.

I poured a jar of Sage's homemade tomato sauce over the beef and pork mixture when "Medicina de Amor" by Raulín Rodríguez came on.

"Wow . . . this song brings back memories," I murmured as I stirred, my hips moving to the bongo drums.

Sage, like me, had a diverse taste in music, but favored Bachata and Salsa. It reminded her of her grandparents and her time spent in the Caribbean. This music reminded me of my childhood Sunday mornings. I knew cleaning day had begun when mom turned the stereo all the way up, as if playing music for the entire street.

I heard my phone vibrate on the counter. It was Jonathan.

"Can you watch this for a minute, Sage? My brother-in-law is calling."

"Of course, go on," she said as she waved me off, dancing by herself in the kitchen.

I answered as I headed for my bedroom. "Hey, Jon!"

"Em! How are you, Sis?" his tone was chipper, as always.

"I'm doing well, making some lasagna."

"Ugh, so jealous. How are you liking the Airbnb?"

"It's great. I've made friends with the host. She's incredibly kind and has made me feel welcome."

"That's a relief . . ." he said, trailing off.

"So, what's up?"

"It's Daniela. The wedding planning has not gone as expected, and she's pretty upset. I am trying to be there for her, but I suspect she needs a woman to talk to . . . I was wondering if you'd be willing to come over tomorrow?"

"Yes! Absolutely. Send me your address. I'm doing some job hunting in the morning, so say about noon?"

"Yeah, that's perfect. Thanks, Em." His relieved tone made me smile. I could imagine how helpless he felt with all the wedding stuff.

We hung up and I sat on my bed. The smile on my face still hadn't faded. I thought back to that weekend years ago. I found my wedding dress on a Sears clearance rack. It was a white dress with spaghetti straps and little flowers embroidered at the hem.

It fit me like a glove.

When Nate saw me in it, his sexy smirk appeared, and he began to blush.

"Beautiful . . ." he greeted, that smirk turning into a full smile.

"Lord Nathan! Shall we marry on this fine day?" I had asked, admiring his suit. He had purchased it for our upcoming graduation.

He wrapped me in his arms and hugged me tighter than he ever had before.

Then he whispered into my ear.

"You and me, Beautiful . . . forever."

INTERLUDE
EVA

August 1988

Everyone's breaking point looks a little different.

Eva's came on a three-strike kind of day.

As soon as she stepped into her apartment with her young daughter, she sensed it was the end. The landlord came by shortly after they arrived to place an eviction notice on the door, and her panic set in.

Eva had spent months searching for an apartment in this town. She had heard the schools in this area were among the best, and knew that with just a little patience, she would find something she could afford. When her coworker at the factory told her about a unit she'd seen, a second-floor apartment in a Victorian era home on the South Shore, she was elated.

It was a studio apartment with a small kitchen and bathroom to the left; the remaining space had a paneled partition down the middle to separate the living from the sleeping area. Although small, she could make it work. Emilia's toddler bed fit on one side, and her bedroom set took up the rest of the space.

Now, she stood amongst the ruins, feeling utterly defeated. There were holes in every wall and the partition was destroyed. The mirrored headboard was shattered; he had even destroyed her trinket collection.

Strike one.

Eva was tired of having to start over. She had spent months trying to build something for her little family. After paying household bills and sending money back to her home country to feed her parents, she pinched every remaining penny in hopes of a better life. So much effort, just for Pablo to destroy it all in one night.

His inner turmoil magnified when he began using hard drugs. Eva used to fear his drunken tirades, but now they paled in comparison to his crack use. When he was high, he didn't just get angry . . .

He got evil.

The things he had done to her over the last couple of months could land him in jail for a very long time.

But she chose to ignore her gut and forgive him. Whenever he came down from his paranoia, he would beg forgiveness on his hands and knees, tears flowing, and promise that he wouldn't touch the stuff ever again.

Pablo would get clean for a week or two, start working again, replace all the broken furniture, and even make dinner or help clean the house. He was also more attentive with Emilia. He would help her practice her numbers and letters, then take her to the mall so she could ride the merry go round.

Then, he would disappear again. His reappearance always looked like this; a tornado ravaging everything in sight.

The previous night, Eva had been called in to work a graveyard shift, which she accepted, as it would provide a nice cushion for the holiday season.

And, again, Pablo was nowhere to be found.

Suspecting he was off getting high somewhere, she left Emilia with her brother and went to work. Around two a.m., her landlord called the factory to notify her that he had called the cops on Pablo after he vandalized the apartment. In the past, she would have left work early to post his bail.

This time, she went back to work.

She now realized that despite her efforts to save money, she would have to deplete savings to rebuild . . . again.

As she swept up the broken glass on the floor, she heard the faint sound of crying. She walked toward the bedroom and noticed Emilia crouched in the corner of the room, whimpering quietly.

"Emilia?" she bent down to look at her, "Mami, what's wrong?" She noticed Emilia's bloody finger. "Ay, no, Mija, what happened?"

"I picked up my barbie and this poked me." Emilia held up the jagged end of a glass pipe. Nausea roiled in Eva's stomach when she realized what it was.

Strike Two.

Without another word, she carried her little girl to the kitchen to clean and bandage her cut. Emilia had learned early on that crying would only make things worse, so she was never one to make a scene.

"Muy bien, Emilia. You stayed calm like a big girl. How about we grab your favorites—a chicken sandwich, some noodle soup, and a lollipop?"

Emilia smiled and nodded excitedly.

Eva was determined to distract Emilia from everything she had witnessed that day. As they approached the local bodega, the smell of fresh baked Cuban bread floated from the exhaust vents. Inside, the owner—a middle-aged man with a mustache—was chopping chicken at a cutting board and looked up to greet them. As soon as his eyes landed on Eva, however, his face morphed, and tension quickly filled the space.

"I've been waiting to see when you'd show your face," he spat.

"Excuse me?" Eva asked.

He reached into a drawer, then tossed what he had retrieved over the counter at Eva's feet. "Tell that husband of yours to not come back here until he has my money. I have no use for an expired passport."

"I don't understand, how do you know my husband? Why would he ask you for money . . . and why would you give it to him?"

"He came in here one morning with a sob story about how she," he jabbed a finger at Emilia, "was in the hospital and he needed twenty bucks to buy her medicine. He left his passport here as collateral."

Eva's jaw set as she fought back her emotions. Even as her eyes pooled with tears, she forbid them to shed. This unkind man would not get the satisfaction. She bent down to grab Pablo's passport. She then pulled a twenty-dollar bill from her wallet—money she had been saving for Christmas— and placed it on the counter.

"Vámonos, Emilia." She grabbed her young daughter's hand. "We aren't welcome here."

Strike Three.

6

STARSTRUCK

I checked my emails again . . . nothing.

Over the past few days, I'd submitted online applications to a plethora of different places, but still hadn't received a response. I didn't really care where I worked, as I knew it would be temporary until I got settled and figured out my next steps.

Regardless, I felt good, relaxed, even. That scared me. I had never been a relaxed person, and feared my restlessness would return with a vengeance.

Jonathan's ranch style home was just a few minutes from Raquel's place. I never understood why he came back to our hometown after he was discharged; it was his chance to escape this island and explore the world. My best guess was that he didn't want to leave his mom alone.

The little, white home sat on a cul de sac and had just one big tree on the side. I knocked on the front door but heard a shout coming from the backyard.

"Em, come around back!" Jonathan's voice boomed.

I walked around and opened the gate, where I found Jonathan struggling to keep his German Shepard contained. He was trying to keep Oliver from tackling me to the ground. Not because he was aggressive, on the contrary, Oliver was my bud. I had met him as a puppy when Jonathan still lived in his apartment. I could tell he remembered me. His tail wagged so violently, I'm sure Jonathan felt like he was being whipped. Now, he was almost as big as me and his excitement was palpable.

"Sorry, Em. Daniela is in the shower, and Oliver does not want to go inside."

"It's okay," I said as I approached, "I once learned from a former client who worked as a dog trainer, that if I approach calmly, and ignore incorrect behavior right away, a dog should correct course and calm down."

Once I reached them, I slowly extended my hand, which Oliver desperately licked. When he tried to jump, I quickly turned my back to him, then waited for him to obey Jonathan's command. When he complied, I cooed at him while I rubbed his face. Before I knew it, Jonathan let go and Oliver stayed by my side.

"Look at you, dog whisperer," Jonathan mused.

"I think I just found my next career," I laughed.

He poured me some lemonade, and we sat on the back patio while we waited for Daniela to come out. We talked about all the work he had put into the home since he purchased it a year ago. I didn't expect to learn so much about miter saws and their many functions.

I did, however, realize that Jonathan was attempting to smother me with small talk. There was something else on his mind, and he likely didn't know how to approach the subject. Eventually I ripped the Band-Aid off and asked him to shoot straight.

"If you don't want to talk about this, I get it . . . I just want to know why you two split. I mean, if anyone was going to last, we thought it was going to be you."

I searched for an uncomplicated response. "I lost Nathan a long time ago. I miss him, but I don't think I'll find him again."

His eyes brightened, hope flashing across his face. "He's just a phone call away, Em. Seriously, he texts me all the time to check on you."

I smiled weakly. "No . . . I miss the *old* Nate. The Nate I married. He became so cold and distant. A wall was built, and I didn't realize it until it was too late. He and I spent so much time at work, you'd think we'd miss each other, but the years passed . . . and everything felt so transactional. He never seemed to want to do anything together. I'd try to plan a getaway, or something romantic, but he always had to work. I would invite him out to work functions or back up north to visit y'all . . . nothing. He was so withdrawn, and I realized that I was in that relationship alone."

Jonathan nodded intently. "Nate disconnected from everyone over the years. Mom still resents him for getting married so young and leaving the state."

I had very strong opinions about Nate and Jonathan's mother, all of them unsavory. "Is he coming up for the wedding?" I asked while stirring my lemonade.

When Jonathan hesitated, I looked up from my glass, "Jon?"

"He is . . ." he muttered.

I chuckled at his meek expression. "Why do you say it like that?"

"He didn't want me to tell you."

"Why?"

"My guess, is that he didn't want his presence to discourage you from attending."

I rolled my eyes. "Please. We aren't children."

"Then why won't you talk to him, Emilia?" A soft accusation, but an accusation, nevertheless.

"Because I wouldn't know what to say," I admitted. I didn't want to pour salt on any wounds.

Just then, the back door swung open, and Daniela stepped outside, much to my relief.

"Emilia! How are you!" Daniela squealed as she embraced me.

I was short, but she was tiny! She had long black hair that reached the base of her back and olive skin like my own. A pretty beauty mark adorned her upper lip. This girl had curves for days. As she headed for a chair, Jonathan patted his thigh and pouted at her. She rolled her eyes as a giggle escaped her, then she sat on his lap.

I felt a sinking feeling. Nate used to do that with me, in front of Jonathan at times. I wondered if it was a learned behavior.

"Dani, I invited Em over because you've been stressed out with the wedding. I thought some female perspective might be helpful."

Daniela's face fell. "Ay, Em . . . everything feels so bittersweet. My mom and my sisters can't be here to help me pick out a dress or organize anything. I don't have a lot of female friends, just a cousin who lives nearby, so as of now, I barely have a bridal party!"

"Did their visa applications get denied?" I asked.

"No, but the wait time is over twenty-four months! We can't wait that long to get married. And given the current political climate, I don't want to request parole and risk not being allowed to return." Her lips began to quiver.

Daniela is a Dreamer. She migrated with her family from Mexico as a baby and was raised here, but her family returned to Mexico a while back.

My heart broke for her.

She was very close to her family. It was a humble, tight-knit family, with a hard-working father, a doting mother, and four energetic girls that worked tirelessly to make their parents proud. Daniela was the only one that was granted Dreamer status; everyone else had to go back.

I was going to suggest that they marry in Mexico, but it suddenly occurred to me that she *also* couldn't travel to see her family. My mother had faced similar challenges when she only had a worker's permit. Decades had passed before she could go back and visit my grandmother. Jonathan rubbed her back and held her hand.

He is going to make an excellent husband, I thought.

I walked over and bent down in front of her. "Don't worry, Honey. Whatever you need, I am here for you."

She laughed in between sniffles. "So, you'll be my matron of honor?"

I smiled. "If you want me to be?"

"Wait . . . Seriously? I was joking . . . but you'd really do it?"

"Why not?"

Jonathan and Daniela looked at each other in surprise.

"Em, Nate's my best man . . . you'd be walking down the aisle with him."

"Wouldn't be the first time," I quipped. We all burst into laughter.

"So, when are we going dress shopping?" I asked.

"I'm free now?" Her eyes lit up like fireworks.

"I had planned to take my mom to lunch . . . would you mind if she joins us?

"Not at all, the more the merrier! I'll grab my bag!" she jumped off Jonathan's lap and headed for the door.

Relieved, Jonathan gave my hand a squeeze. "Thanks, Sis."

The dress shopping experience was eye opening for all three of us.

My mom had remarried later in life and wore a shimmery, white maxi dress for her beach wedding. I had gotten married in a pretty summer dress off a sales rack.

Daniela was going to be a princess.

When we arrived at the bridal shop, we were greeted by eager bridal consultants who put us in a large dressing area and served us champagne.

The three of us had completely different ideas for which dress style she should try on. Daniela wanted an empire waist, while my mom wanted her to try a ball gown with a lot of lace and beading. I thought she should show off her curves in a mermaid gown.

"But pick whatever you want, Honey. You will know when you have the right one," I reminded her.

"Whatever you pick," Mom interjected, "the veil needs to be looooong."

They whisked Daniela away to try on the first dress when I noticed my mom looking around the store and avoiding my gaze.

"Mami, you're being weird ... what's up?" I asked.

"Nada," she said as she played with her purse strap.

Nada, never meant Nada. I waited for her to finish.

"It would have been nice to do this with you. You deserved to get married the *right* way."

I withheld my exasperation. "What was the right way, Mom?"

"In a church, with God's blessing. With your parents there, to give you away."

"We didn't even go to church!"

"That's not the point. There is a right way to do things, Mija. I had to hear it from everyone when you ran off with Nathan. My family and your father's family both blamed me for what you did."

I bit my tongue so hard I could taste blood. I would not ruin this special day arguing with her.

"Okay, Mom," I whispered, just as Daniela came out in the first empire gown.

The top was a tight lace bodice with scalloped edging and mini sleeves. The front had jeweled embroidery with a long-pleated skirt. It was a beautiful dress.

But it was all wrong.

Daniela took one look at it, and I could tell she wasn't impressed. She then turned around.

"Be honest," she instructed.

I started gently. "If you feel beautiful, we should definitely explore more in this style."

I followed her gaze over to my mom, who looked like someone stuck an anchovy under her nose.

"Mom," I chastised. "Fix your face ... Jeez."

"I'm sorry," she said to Daniela while shaking her head. "You are gorgeous, Mija. But this dress it not the one. You look pregnant."

"Oh my god, Mami, stop—"

"Which wouldn't be an issue if you *were* pregnant, but you're not, so it's a problem."

I looked over to the consultant who was battling shock and disappointment at my mom's blunt criticism, then we all turned to look at Daniela.

When she threw her head back and laughed, we all sighed in relief. She was grabbing her stomach and had to wipe her tears.

"Ay, Doña Eva. That made my day. That is totally something my mom would say."

"Pues, es verdad," my mom chuckled.

She seemed okay with switching gears and tried several styles, even ones she hadn't previously considered. I was worried she'd get discouraged after trying on her tenth gown, but she seemed enjoy herself. She had probably been worried she wouldn't get to experience this at all.

She tried some mermaid gowns, which looked phenomenal on her, but said they were too provocative for her taste. She indulged my mom and tried every Catholic, 90s-style gown the shop had. They were beautiful, sure, but too extravagant. She was having a small ceremony, so she wanted something to fit the bill.

Finally, she stepped out, and our jaws dropped. She had selected an A-line, satin gown with lace over a sweetheart neckline and mini sleeves. The back was lace that swooped down into a button closure. She had a long lace veil trailing behind her.

She was breathtaking.

When she stepped onto the platform and saw herself, I

thought she was going to faint. My mom quietly dabbed at her tears, while I held mine back.

She turned around and we both just nodded back at her, our smiles wide and proud.

"Now that's more like it," Mom said.

At lunch, I convinced Daniela to allow me to do her hair and makeup as my wedding gift. She resisted at first, but once I showed her pictures of some of my bridal clients, she caved. We made a to-do list and assigned the tasks she could delegate to me, so she could focus on the big-ticket items—like *where* they were getting married.

"I've narrowed it down to a couple of spots, one is on the water near where you live. I just need to make a decision."

"That one is important, Honey. March will be here in no time," I reminded her.

"Doña Eva, can I ask a big favor?" Daniela looked at her nervously. "Could I have you stand in for my mother during the ceremony? I know its unconventional, but I don't want our pictures to look uneven with only Jon's mom there."

"Of course, Mija! No se preocupe; we've got you covered."

Overcome with emotion, she thanked us for supporting her. She also shared her plans upon her return visit to Mexico. "Get your passports ready!" Daniela exclaimed, "As soon as I can travel, we will have a church ceremony so my parents can formally give me away. Then, there will be a huge wedding reception, and we will redo all the pictures to include my family!"

"¿Ves?" Mom looked at me with a smug grin. "That's how it's done."

I rolled my eyes. We didn't have a big family waiting for us in another country. I didn't have a father to give me away. Even if I wanted to do all those things, it couldn't never be.

Daniela interjected. "Do you think Raquel would mind being a bridesmaid? I know I've only met her a couple of times, but I'll pay for everything she needs!"

"Are you kidding?" I laughed. "Raquel loves to party. I'll give you her number so you two can talk details."

I took Daniela home, then headed for Mom's house. I pulled into the driveway, then put the car in park. I really hoped she wouldn't ask me to come inside. "It was very sweet of you to accept Daniela's request," I said.

"Yeah, she's a great girl. Besides, it will be nice to do it at least once." She stared out the window.

I didn't take the bait. I'd been explaining my actions for years, I was tired.

"See you at Thanksgiving dinner, Mom," I said before putting the car in reverse.

Sage lit a few candles on the windowsill while I straightened the couch pillows. Even though Friendsgiving was a small affair, I was still nervous. There were several new faces coming, and Will would be in attendance. I had sensed a spark when we met and was cautiously optimistic.

I may have separated from Nate, but I was still married. I was trepidatious at the mere thought of entertaining a spark.

I walked over to the buffet Sage had laid out, which she adorned with wildflowers, acorns, and multicolored corn husks. She mentioned she always sought out Indigenous and Latin American restaurants to cater for Friendsgiving. This was her way of paying homage to their communities during the holiday season. There were roasted meats, rice and wild grains, a large variety of root vegetables, tamales, and corn porridge.

She set the ambience with both flameless and real candles all over the living area; so many that there was no need for overhead lighting.

It was intimate. *Romantic . . .*

I rushed downstairs to check my hair and makeup again. I wore loose French braids and left my long bangs out to frame my face. It complimented my turtleneck and jumpsuit very nicely.

When the doorbell rang, I answered and met a few of Sage's other friends. Stefany was an immigration attorney who just moved her practice from northern Manhattan to the South Shore. Romero was a contractor who specialized in commercial construction and was dabbling in custom home design. Osvaldo was my favorite. A marvelous and flamboyant character, he grew up in Georgia and had the peachiest accent. He moved to New York City in his youth to pursue modeling and eventually settled into makeup artistry.

All of them had one thing in common. They had rented a property from Sage at one point, fell in love with her, and had been close friends ever since.

"That's her MO, Emilia," Osvaldo said. "She charms you with her amazing design taste, then she serves you that witch's brew she calls tea, and boom! You're hooked."

Raquel joined soon after and we played Pictionary while the remaining guests arrived.

She and I never really socialized together outside of family events, so it was nice to see her interact with new people. We were both quick-witted, a characteristic she says we got from our father. I wouldn't know.

I stepped away to grab some roasted pork and an Alcapurria, when I noticed Sage had laid out info cards about each dish.

"Her creativity is something else, isn't it?"

I jumped at the sound of Will's voice. I hadn't even heard him come in.

He laughed at my expression. "I didn't mean to startle you."

"It's okay, I was so engrossed in the cards, I didn't hear anything. How are you?"

He sighed, slipping his hands into his pockets. "Well, I met someone last week, and have been thinking about her ever since."

"Is that so?" I asked, dumping more food on my plate in an attempt to avert his gaze.

"Yeah . . . It was quite distracting, but I'm all better now."

I didn't know what to say. Men have tried to flirt with me in the past, but a quick flash of my wedding ring, and they'd scurry off. I didn't wear my band anymore, and I wasn't sure I wanted Will to go anywhere.

Before I had a chance to respond, Raquel came into the kitchen. "Emi, what's taking you so long—Oh, hello!" she said to Will, "I'm Raquel, Emilia's sister."

"I'm Will," he said with a bright smile. "Beauty runs in the family, Emilia," he added.

"Well, aren't you a charmer," Raquel's skin warmed as she looked back at me. Will excused himself and walked back to the living room. I could feel Raquel's laser focus on my back. "Emilia Contreras," she said with an emphasis on my married name, "who is that . . . and are you even ready to find out?"

Normally tickled by her wanting to mother me, I found myself annoyed. I spun around and faced her.

"His name is Will; he is Andrea's son." I pointed to Andy on the couch. "I met him at her boutique the day we had lunch. And I'm not sure whether I'm *ready* to find out, but I'll be making that decision on my own. Okay?" I tried to keep my tone as light as possible, but there was an edge and she picked up on it.

Raquel threw her hands up in the air. "Okay. Sheesh. Sorry for asking; any who, Daniela called me earlier to ask me to be in her wedding. That was a doozy!" She giggled as she threw a grape in her mouth. "I told her I'd love to."

"I told her you wouldn't turn down the opportunity to dress up and party."

We both laughed, then put our game faces on and headed back to the living room.

⸺

Friendsgiving was the most fun I'd had in a very long time. Sage was an excellent host—not a surprise to anyone—and had us all laughing, crying, and singing most of the evening.

She even brought out her guitar and sat cross-legged in the middle of her living room floor, taking song requests. Andy's singing abilities were well known to the group, but Raquel and I were blown away. There was a richness, a pain in her voice. Andy's voice seemed to transcend our space, as if she sang on behalf of those who came before her.

Will was charming, indeed. He kept everyone laughing and would not let the conversation die out. Aside from being handsome, there was a warmth about him—he wore his heart on his sleeve, and it was refreshing to see a man unafraid to express his emotions.

Before I knew it, hours had passed, and it was time to wrap up. After exchanging numbers, Stefany and Romero promised to plan another outing—maybe head into the city and watch a show on Broadway—then they left. Osvaldo and I set a lunch date in the following weeks.

Raquel gave me a kiss and reminded me she'd see me at my mom's house for Thanksgiving. She walked over to Sage who hugged her tight for what seemed like hours, then told her to stop by whenever she wished.

Andy, Will, and I helped Sage clean up and I figured I should excuse myself for the evening.

"Oh no you don't." Sage wagged a finger at me, "There's an after party!"

I laughed, but quickly realized she wasn't joking. "Are there more guests coming?"

She shook her head. "We are going to show you the Bluff tonight. I have some hot cocoa ready, and the blankets are packed."

I could not contain my excitement. I'd been looking forward to seeing the Bluff since they first mentioned it.

"We have clear skies tonight, so the view of the stars will be spectacular," Andy smiled.

I ran and grabbed my coat.

The Bluff did not disappoint.

How Sage got a key to the side gate was anyone's guess. She had probably charmed a park ranger into letting her in after hours.

After she locked the gate behind her, we drove down a short, winding road to a little cove that was hidden from public view. The shore was rocky, and there were logs positioned in a square, with a fire pit in the middle. The trees hung over head, with one in particular calling my attention.

"It's a contorted beech," Sage explained. "This one is special as its flowers blossom in different colors."

I felt a familiar wave of energy come over me. This place, this hidey spot, gave off a healing vibe. Like it invites you to stay so it can nurse your soul back to health. Will and Andy brought some firewood from the trunk and began to set the fire while Sage and I laid out the blankets.

"Okay, Emi. I want you to close your eyes and lay on your back," Sage instructed.

"Okay . . ." I laughed nervously.

"Now, open your eyes," she gently coaxed.

The moment my eyes opened I was overwhelmed with sensation. My nostrils flared as they inhaled the ocean's briny scent. My ears not only heard the waves, my body absorbed the vibration of their crash against the sand.

And my eyes . . .

I'd never seen the stars so clearly before. Hundreds, thousands of twinkling jewels hung in the sky. Not one more beautiful than the other. To think that they were on display all the time, and we just didn't notice them, was tragic.

"Wow," I whispered as tears traveled down the sides of my face. "There are no words . . ."

"No, there aren't," Will said. I turned my head to the side and noticed the three staring up at the sky, equally entranced with the star show. Will looked down at me then, his emotions on full display. There was so much tenderness in his eyes. They communicated his interest, and it felt nice to be wanted. I smiled back, letting him know we were on the same page, but first, I had to tie up some loose ends.

It was time to write Nate back.

7

WHO WOULDN'T GO?

We haven't had an emergency session in a while, Ann thought as she watched Nathan pace the room with hands on his hips. She took notice of his drastic physical transformation over the past couple of months. In all the years she had known him, he had been slim, even gaunt if he was in a depressive state; a tell-tale sign that he was in crisis.

It was obvious that he was taking his health and fitness seriously nowadays. His broad shoulders had grown, and his arms now filled out his shirt. She quickly re-centered before she could venture past a professional observation.

"Nathan?" Ann gently asked. "Why don't you try sitting down for a moment and talk me through your thoughts?"

He sat down, then took a couple of deep breaths. "Emilia wrote back," he managed before another long exhale. "Shall I read it to you?"

Ann nodded for him to proceed. He pulled the letter out of his back pocket and unfolded the paper. His expression said it all; this wasn't the response he wanted.

Nathan,

While I appreciate your apology, I'm afraid it's too late. I've made the decision to move on, and while it may be hard to believe, it's not because I don't love you.

I do.

Life is too short, and we all deserve the opportunity to thrive. Together, we got stuck. I am hoping that apart, we can move forward.

I know there is a mandatory separation period before we can finalize everything.

Regardless, you are free.

Emilia

He paused for a moment, as if his eyes couldn't believe what he had just read, before crushing the paper in his fist.

"I don't know what to do with this, Ann," he whispered, as he held his head in his hands.

"This isn't the response you'd hoped for, but now that you've got it, help me understand what you are feeling."

He scoffed. "I struggle with expressing myself in words. I can only describe what I want to do with the pain."

"Which is?"

He sighed. "Surprisingly, not what I've wanted to do in the past. The overwhelming need to disappear isn't there. But I am hurting. I miss her so much. I know I spent the past few years guarded . . . still, she was loyal, and I loved and respected her for it.

I've spent the last couple of months working on myself, and I'd be lying if I said it wasn't for her. I was hoping that when she came around, she'd find a new and improved Nate. One she could be proud of. Now I feel like it was all a waste."

Before Ann could stop herself, a snicker escaped her.

Nate looked up in surprise. "Something funny?" he asked. He didn't seem offended, just surprised.

"I apologize. It was a knee-jerk response, but inappropriate, nevertheless. I can assure you it wasn't at your expense . . . you just made two paradoxical statements."

"How so?"

"First, you said you couldn't express your feelings in words, but I'd argue that you did a fantastic job doing just that. You should be proud, Nathan. You've come a long way since the first time we met."

"Thank you," Nate smirked, his cheeks flushed. It was clear that he wasn't used to positive reinforcement.

"Then, you mentioned that you began this self-improvement journey 'for her.' It's ironic how hard we will work toward something when we've convinced ourselves it's for someone else's benefit. Really, you've just created the *idea* that it's for her. All along, you've pursued your goal based on a hope, with no real guarantee. So, what—now that she's seemingly moving on, a new and improved Nate isn't worth it? What if *Nate* wants a new and improved Nate? Emilia was right when she said we all deserve the opportunity to thrive."

Nate nodded, a pensive glaze crossing his eyes. "I'm going to New York in a few months for my brother's wedding. We've been texting each other and have had a few conversations over the phone. I am trying to reconnect with him."

Ann nodded while making a note to ask about the brother in their next session.

"I'll likely see Emilia at the wedding . . . and my mother. So, you and I have just a few months to make sure I am good to go up here," he said, tapping his temple.

"I'm up for the challenge, but I think you'll do just fine." Ann smiled.

Nate had just come home from the gym and was about to whip up a protein shake when his cell phone chimed. His colleague, Carl, had sent him details for Thanksgiving dinner; an invite he gladly accepted.

He usually spent the holidays alone. Emilia used to go back up north to spend the holidays with her family, and he worked to stay busy. He now realized how neglected Emilia must have felt throughout the years. In the early days, she would do her best to make the house festive and create happy holiday memories. He was jaded. Nate's childhood memories around the holidays were some of his worst.

This year, he wouldn't have work as an excuse, so Carl and his lovely wife Francine would be a welcome distraction. Carl was the one person at work Nate actually liked and respected. He even felt comfortable enough to open up to him about his marital troubles.

After feeding Capri and cuddling with her on the couch, he jumped in the shower. Expecting the tears to come, he leaned his head against the shower door. He'd spent countless evenings letting his sorrows out in that exact spot, hoping the water would drown out the sound of his cries. Surprisingly, the tears didn't come. His heart ached at the thought of never having another chance with Emilia. He was upset about her decision but knew deep down she was right.

She deserved happiness.

He decided he would respect her wishes and let fate decide what the future held for them. So much time had been wasted, and he also wanted a chance to thrive.

Not again . . .

The tears ran down the sides of my face as I stared at the ceiling, but I felt hollow. For the first time in over a month, I dreamt of my father. Instead of a flashback, I had a similar dream to what Raquel described. He would smile at me, then open his mouth to say something, but no sound would come out. I could hear myself asking him to speak louder, but it was like he was muted.

When I came to, my face was wet from tears, and I instantly felt sick. The dream was likely triggered by seeing my family at Thanksgiving dinner the night before.

My mom hosted Thanksgiving at her house every year. Raquel and Marta were always invited, so Raquel was accustomed to spending the holiday there as well. The food was delicious as always, and Mom was in great spirits. Her husband was such a doting man, and I was elated to finally see her happy . . . and safe. There was loud music, enthusiastic karaoke, and a boisterous uncle or cousin in the corner somewhere, not making any sense anymore.

Raquel was her usual chipper self and brought up stories about our father several times, which my mom listened to graciously. After dinner and clean up, Raquel laid on the couch and threw her head on my lap.

"Emi, we should video chat with Grandma," she said.

I grimaced. "Do we have to?"

"Yes. We won't hear the end of it if we don't call." She pulled out her phone and dialed.

My grandmother replied on the first ring.

"Aha! I was wondering when my granddaughters would call." My grandmother's greeting was exactly what I expected. Raquel laughed it off and quickly distracted her before she could continue.

"We just got done eating and helping Eva clean up. What did you eat?" she asked.

Raquel's jovial tone was irking the hell out of me. I understand being cordial, but there was no need to brown nose so much.

"Sara dropped some food off for me."

"You didn't go to Tia's house for dinner?" Raquel asked, her brows furrowed.

"I'm not in a celebratory mood this year. I am in mourning." Her tone was pointed. I could hear the silent *"as you should be"* hang in the air.

"I understand, Abuela," Raquel said.

"Emilia, you haven't said anything, are you okay?" she asked.

I tried to keep my tone light. I really had no desire to speak to her but was too spineless to say so, especially on a holiday. "I'm fine, Abuela. Just listening to the conversation."

"Okay . . ." she said, clearly not convinced, "well remember something—your dad died, not me. You can call from time to time, I don't bite."

Oh, yes you do.

"I know . . . I'm going to go help my mom finish cleaning up. You get some rest, and we'll catch up at Christmas, okay?"

"Okay, Mija, take care of yourself," she said as I walked away.

Raquel stayed on the phone and reminisced about our father for a while longer. When I looked back over, I noticed her packing up to leave. She said her goodbyes to my family, and I walked her to her car. "Come over next week and we can brainstorm about some of Daniela's wedding tasks, okay?"

"Yeah, Flaca. I'll call you," I said looking down at my shoes.

"Emi, what's wrong?" she asked.

Interacting with our grandmother makes me uncomfortable and I'm still a little mad at you.

"Nothing, I think something upset my stomach," I quickly replied.

She eyed me for a moment, then accepted my answer. As she drove away, I felt my phone vibrate in my back pocket.

It was Will.

So much to be grateful for . . . I'm especially thankful that you agreed to dinner tomorrow.

I smiled. After sending a quick reply I went back inside and enjoyed the rest of the evening.

A couple of days after our night at the Bluff, Sage had traveled to LA to spend time with friends, so the house was quiet, as if it lay dormant, waiting for its energy source to return. I kept up with her plants and made sure her impeccably clean house remained tidy.

The morning after Thanksgiving, my anxiety was at a ten. This would happen to me regularly in North Carolina, and housework was my usual remedy. I'd clean for hours until I either calmed down or was too exhausted to continue; whichever came first. I grabbed some supplies out of Sage's utility room and gave my bathroom a deep clean. Then, I reorganized my wardrobe by color. I hated the result, so I tried to sort again by occasion, hated that, then reverted to color again.

After carefully examining every article of clothing I owned, I decided to purchase a new outfit for my date with Will.

A shopping trip on Black Friday? Huge mistake.

The department store looked like a natural disaster site. Clothes and shoes were out of place everywhere. The associates already looked worn out, and it was only ten a.m. I lucked out and found a dark mauve sweater dress that hit me mid-thigh. When I tried it on, it hugged my curves perfectly.

Amazed by my good fortune, I decided to knock out my Christmas list. I spent more time waiting in lines to check out than I did to find the gifts.

Desperate to escape the pandemonium, I grabbed some lunch to-go and headed home.

While driving, I received a call from Osvaldo.

"Hey, Os!"

"Darlin! Listen, I know we only met a week ago, but we are basically sisters now, right?"

I laughed. "I've always wanted another sister, so yeah! What's up?"

"I have a huge favor to ask you. We have two clients that are getting married next week, a few days apart. They're sisters that both wanted a winter ceremony and decided to marry within the same week instead of making family and friends travel twice in a month . . ."

"Oof! Thoughtful, but a lot of work," I remarked.

"Our sentiments, exactly. The hair stylist, a dear friend of mine, contracted me to do makeup, but there was a sudden death in her family, and she won't make it. All of our mutuals are booked, and I fear we won't find someone in time! Then, I remembered the pictures you showed me of your clients and thought I'd shoot my shot . . ."

Ah, yes, there it is.

"Would you like me to step in?" I asked gently.

"If you don't, I'll die, I swear I will!" His melodramatic responses were my favorite part about him. He added, "Seriously though, if the hair trials go well, my friend will pay you double her rate per head."

I didn't need much coaxing. I was beginning to feel restless and needed to occupy my time. Besides, I looked forward to playing with some hair again, and I particularly enjoyed bridal hairstyles.

"Okay, count me in!" I exclaimed.

"You are an angel, Emilia." He took a long sigh, "After the trials, shall we do lunch?"

"You bet. Send me the details, and I'll see you then."

"Talk soon, love."

We hung up and I ate lunch while I watched House M.D. reruns on my tablet. Before I knew it, it was time to get ready, so I headed for the shower. I shaved my legs for the first time since I moved back. Fall and winter were no-shave seasons for me, but I couldn't help myself. Even though I was wearing sheer tights and over-the-knee heeled boots, I wouldn't feel put together unless I had smooth legs.

I let out my fresh blowout and parted my hair to one side. It was shiny and full of bounce. My makeup was soft and sleepy. I had to admit, I looked hot. Somewhere in the deep recesses of my mind a little voice whispered, *Eat your heart out, Nate.*

I shook the thought off and put on my boots.

Will was at the door to pick me up at exactly seven p.m. I'd be lying if I said I wasn't thrilled to see his reaction to my outfit.

"Good God, Emilia," he muttered as he looked me up and down. When his eyes met mine, he smiled so wide, my first instinct was to retreat. Will was very expressive, and it could be overwhelming at times.

"Am I overdressed?" I asked as I took in his turtleneck and jeans.

"Yes *and* no." His words took a second to register, and I felt heat rush to my face. His eyes were like a flame of fire, warm and intense. Dangerous, yet alluring.

Without another word, he grabbed my hand and walked me to the car, then opened my door.

The restaurant was a short drive, which was one of my favorite parts of being back on Long Island. There were so many great, privately owned restaurants, for all occasions. The Tapas Bar had a heated patio that was decorated beautifully with high lattice walls covered in moss, and string lights to provide ambient lighting. The candle lit tables and fresh flowers made for a very romantic setting. Half a bottle of wine and several tapas later, we were laughing nonstop.

Will was so easy to talk to. He was open-minded, curious, and had a fiery spirit. He loved to dance and travel; all things I wanted to experience myself. We briefly discussed my situation with Nate, and he was very understanding. The only topic he didn't feel comfortable discussing was his ex-girlfriend. When I inquired, he averted my gaze and kept his responses vague.

"She wasn't the one, Emilia," he said as he sipped his wine.

I took the hint and dropped the subject.

After dinner, we went to a club where a local singer was performing an Etta James tribute. Her voice was fantastic.

"But she's not as good as your mother, Will. Andy can sing!"

His warm laugh made my stomach jump. "Why she never pursued a career in music is beyond me. Andy is my stepmom, you know . . ."

"Oh, I didn't realize. I figured you were mixed."

"I am. Dad was white, Mom was Dominican; both passed when I was young. Dad married Andy a year before he passed away. I was six years old."

"Oh no! I'm so sorry to hear that." I grabbed his hand, and he kept it fixed on his lap.

"Don't be. Death is a part of life, and I made peace with that a long time ago. Besides, Andy was the best thing that happened to Dad and me. I've learned so much from her."

I smiled softly and noticed that he had no intention of letting go of my hand. We watched the singer deliver the most beautiful rendition of "Trust in Me."

After the tribute concert ended, Will offered to take me back to his place for a nightcap, but I politely declined.

"Nothing good happens after midnight, Will."

"I beg to differ, Emilia," he smiled, his eyes fixed on the road.

I walked right into that one. As tempting as his offer was, he accepted my answer like a gentleman, and walked me to Sage's front door.

Before I had a chance to thank him, he wrapped his hands around my waist and brought me close to him. I looked into his eyes, so warm and gentle. Mesmerized, I leaned in and kissed him.

His lips were warm, and the scent of his cologne intoxicating. He pulled me close to his chest and the kiss swiftly grew in intensity. I could feel his hands running through my hair and a wave of desire washed over me.

Then, in a split second, everything changed. My blood ran cold, and I began to feel suffocated. I disengaged.

"I have to go, Will. Thank you for a lovely evening," I whispered, my hands still on his chest.

Both of us were still catching our breath, and he nodded.

"I'm traveling for work next week, but I'd love to see you when I get back." His fiery eyes studied me.

All I wanted was to crawl into a cave and not come out. These emotions were bubbling to the surface all at once, and I was helpless to stop them. "Okay. Call me when you're back," I murmured.

He smiled, then took my hand from his chest and kissed it, before walking away.

As soon as I was inside, I jumped into the shower and began my nighttime routine. Only when I climbed into bed, did I allow myself to process the evening. That was, by far one of the best kisses I'd ever experienced.

Will's passion seeped from his pores, and he was incredibly sexy. I felt safe with him. Desired. He didn't look past me. He actually saw me. It felt so good to be appreciated.

There was only one problem . . . When my eyes closed and passion took over, all I saw was Nate.

A few days later, I was in Sage's living room unwrapping the most expensive ornaments I'd ever seen.

"You have to tell me everything!" Sage squealed as she fixed ornaments to her garland.

Her holiday theme was black, teal, and gold. She personally celebrated the winter solstice, but still threw holiday parties, again, to no one's surprise. In typical Sage fashion, the décor was plucked out of a magazine. She had multiple frosted trees twinkling throughout the house, and holiday jazz was playing all day. She made Mexican hot chocolate and got tamales from our neighbor down the street. I also loved to decorate and hadn't had the opportunity to do so in years. Nate was never a fan of the holiday season, and after I lost my third baby, everything felt tainted.

As soon as Sage walked through the door a few days ago, the first thing she said to me was, "My doorbell camera caught the steamiest smooch I've ever seen!" Then she did a twirl.

An actual twirl.

I was mortified. It didn't even occur to me that we were standing in front of the camera.

"I promise, I didn't listen to the audio; that felt intrusive. I didn't even watch the whole recording. My friends and I were at a play when the video came through during intermission, so I only caught the preview. Everyone was wondering why I was screaming in the lobby!"

That didn't make me feel any better, but I did give her the rundown about the date. "He's incredibly attractive, smart, and funny." It was hard to keep from smiling.

Sage struggled to contain her excitement. "Will is a great man, Emilia. I approve of this courtship." Her smile was big and I couldn't help but laugh at her seal of approval.

I decided not to mention my dreams with Dad, or my thoughts of Nate.

Once we were done decorating, we caught a movie, and I forced her to let me buy dinner. We agreed that we would begin wedding plans, AKA Operation: Pledge Your Troth, after the holidays wrapped up.

I was excited to have Sage home. It felt like light had entered the home again, and I was looking forward to a peaceful night's rest.

———

"Don't fucking lie to me!" he roars.

The belt lashes me again, and I struggle to hold the book over my head. I'd been kneeling for over an hour, and this time, it is on rice. The grains dig into my skin, and I begin to lose balance. If I drop this book, my father will be furious.

He doesn't typically lose his temper unless he is drunk or high, and he rarely hits us kids, but he has been sick lately, so he is hungover and grumpy. He whips me again, and this time I howl in pain.

Just then, my grandmother comes into the room. "What is going on!" she shouts, looking down at the ground.

I am trying not to cry, but I am shaking from the strain.

He turns to my grandmother. "Her mother called. The school caught her cheating on an exam, and she failed one of her classes.

If she doesn't take summer classes, she doesn't advance to middle school."

He sighs. "You are so ungrateful, Emilia. All the effort I put into buying your school clothes and supplies, just for you to cheat in class."

"I didn't cheat," I whisper, my voice breaking.

"What did I say about lying?" he shouts. Before he can strike me again, my grandmother steps in.

"Why do you have to hit her so much, and what the hell is the matter with you, making her kneel on rice?"

He spins around so quickly, my grandmother flinches. "What did you just say?" he asks, his tone eerie, "Do you remember what you used to make me kneel on? It wasn't rice!" He grabs the bag on the bed and throws it at her. Rice splatters all over her then onto the floor. "It was fucking stones, woman. You would make me kneel on sharp stones, for hours. Then, you'd hit me with a switch until I bled, or my knees gave out. Now, all of a sudden, rice is offensive to you?" He shakes his head, and I can see the anger in his eyes. "Unbelievable! Then, if I don't discipline my kids, you get to talk shit about how I'm not a real man, right?"

He is right about that. She always berates him about being too lenient with me and Raquel, saying us girls need to "be domesticated" so we could grow up to be decent wives and mothers.

My grandmother is no saint. Sometimes she'd hit us just for lounging too long. If she is up doing something, she expects us by her side to help.

"That was a different time, and we are in a different country. You can get in serious trouble for this," she says quietly.

"Fine!" I hear the belt hit the floor, "You fucking deal with her." He storms off.

My grandmother doesn't move until she hears the front door slam. "Put the book down, Emilia," she orders. "Grab a broom and pick this mess up."

I slowly stand and pull up my overalls. My braids are all messed up and I can't stop shaking.

She hangs up the belt in the closet. "This is what happens when careless mothers don't pay attention to their kid's grades."

"Grandma, I didn't cheat."

She spins around and gets in my face. "Are you calling him a liar?" she shouts. She is getting angry, and her hand isn't any better than the belt. "Your dad is right; you are very ungrateful. When you are done, pack your things. I'm dropping you off at your mother's house."

8

SILENT NIGHTS

December 1998

"Is it a new basketball?" Jonathan asked as he shoveled snow onto Nate's side.

"Jon, stop it!" he scolded, "I already told you; I didn't see what was in the bag, just that it was from the sporting goods store. Be grateful you are getting anything at all, you know how last year went. Now let's finish up before Rick comes home."

Their stepfather was a tyrant. Nate never understood why their mom had chosen that asshole. Their dad died when Nate was three years old, so he didn't remember anything about him; their mom was pregnant with Jonathan at the time. Nate did know that he never beat their mom. He remembered a much happier version of her before their stepfather entered their lives. Rick ruled the entire household with his fists; it was his preferred method to keep everyone in line.

Nate and his mother did their best to protect Jonathan from

the violence; normally taking the blame for chores not being done on time or being done incorrectly.

Nate was fourteen and Jonathan's eleventh birthday was quickly approaching. He tried to teach Jonathan not to get too excited. Right before a holiday, Rick would find the smallest reason to punish them for something, thus taking away their gifts or canceling any planned outings.

It was like the bastard got a kick out of punishing everyone. Last year, Nate got a black eye for his birthday, simply for suggesting he could buy a skateboard with his own money. His mom had just stood there and watched, then slowly turned her back and continued doing dishes.

Nate and Jonathan learned to walk on eggshells, but it seemed that no matter how much their mom tried to stay one step ahead of Rick—having dinner ready on time, keeping the house spotless, always looking put together—it didn't save her from the insults or the blows.

He treated everyone in the house with hatred.

One day, while icing his mom's head he asked, "Mom, why doesn't he like us? We haven't done anything wrong . . ."

She always had a ready excuse for his actions. "He's under a lot of stress at work, Nathan. That is why you should never talk back. It sets him off."

When they finished shoveling, he threw rock salt over the pathway and had Jonathan hang the shovels back in their place in the shed. Their mom made them hot chocolate to warm up and gave them each half a sandwich. Rick expected them to eat at their assigned times and nothing more, so she would often sneak smaller meals for them before he got home.

After cleaning their room and doing their homework, they sat at the coffee table to work on a puzzle until they heard Rick's car roll into the driveway. As his footsteps approached, Nate said a prayer that he was in a good mood; the last few days had been relatively peaceful. He walked through the door, and Jonathan immediately looked up to acknowledge him, just like Nate had taught him.

"Hey. The driveway looks good. I didn't slip, like last time," he said, looking at Nate.

He always needed someone to blame for his misfortune. The last time he slipped, he had come home drunk, and the rain made the driveway slick. None of which was their fault, yet they still got the beating of a lifetime.

Just then, their mom came out of the kitchen and greeted Rick, taking his coat and hanging it on the rack.

"What's for dinner?" he asked.

"Pot roast, like you asked," she replied, keeping her tone light.

"You didn't put any of that cumin shit in it, right? It smells like feet in here."

"No, I stuck to the list of spices you gave me."

"It must be the boys then . . ." His fake cackle annoyed the hell out of Nate. "Alright then, let's eat," he declared.

Rick didn't allow for casual conversation at the table. He asked a question and expected a quick response, otherwise one could expect a backhand to the mouth. Just last month, he had hit Jonathan in the nose and drawn blood. Nate could tell he wanted to cry so he squeezed his thigh under the table. It was tight enough for him to understand that crying only made things worse.

The pot roast was okay, but Nate liked it more when she added cumin. She had tried to teach him how to cook, but he was terrible at it, and eventually she had to stop, or Rick would notice their rationed groceries were being wasted. She said a man who could cook was so attractive and was their dad's one redeeming quality. Their mom didn't like to talk about him, or much of anything, really.

"How's the food, Nathan?" Rick asked.

Mediocre.

Everything their mom cooked nowadays tasted bland, but that's how Rick liked it. He asked as if she had used Rick's own special recipe. This guy liked to take credit for everything; everything was always about him.

"It's delicious," Nate murmured as he took another bite.

"How did you do on your history exam?"

"I got an A."

"See, I told you the flash cards would work."

The flashcards didn't work, you dick. It was the late-night study sessions because the welts you gave me wouldn't let me sleep.

"Yeah, they came in handy."

After Nate and Jonathan washed and dried the dishes, wiped the counters, and swept, they went to their room, and Nate quizzed Jonathan on geometry terms. After a few rounds of Uno, Jonathan went to sleep. Nate read a chapter of "Of Mice and Men" before dozing off.

He woke to a loud thud followed by the sound of his mom's cries. He jumped out of bed and quietly opened the door to investigate.

"I don't know why it's not happening, please let go of my hair."

"There is something you aren't telling me, Gloria," he sang with menace. Nate despised his stupid singsong tone.

"I'm getting older, it's not as easy to get pregnant."

"Well, we will just have to try harder, then."

Nate was old enough to understand what was about to happen. He desperately wanted to grab a baseball bat from the garage, kick the door down, and beat the shit out of him with it.

But he knew Rick could still overpower him, and he didn't want his mom or Jon to suffer if Rick won. With bile in his throat, Nate went back to his room and put headphones on. He turned the volume all the way up, in hopes it would drown out the sounds of his mom being raped.

Jonathan never even stirred.

The next day was gloomy, much like his mom's demeanor. Rick went to the gym and would be out most of the day with his "buddies." They never got to go anywhere because he wouldn't let their mom drive.

"Mom?" Nate called as he approached her. She was very jumpy, so he liked to warn her when he came up behind her.

"Yes, Hijo," she murmured while staring out the window.

"Are you okay?" he asked softly.

"Yes, why?" She turned to face him.

"I heard some sounds last ni—"

"It was nothing."

"It didn't sound like nothing . . ."

"Well, it was. And you shouldn't be eavesdropping."

"I wasn't, I was worried about—"

"Stop worrying about me, Nathan!" she shouted. "That is not your job. Your job is protect your brother and not aggravate Rick, do you understand?"

"And who protects you, Mom?" he cried.

She scoffed then wiped her apron. When she looked up, Nate saw just how broken she was.

"No one, Hijo. No one."

———

Bing Crosby's "Have Yourself a Merry Little Christmas" was playing through the speakers while Nate tried to wrap presents. Emilia used to love wrapping presents by the tree. She had patience for these kinds of things.

He did not.

The first issue was, he didn't realize how difficult it was to wrap irregularly shaped objects. Capri wasn't helping matters. Every time he pulled the ribbon out, she wanted to swipe at it. Once she caught it, her predator mode would activate, and it was very distracting. Watching a kitten bunny kick everything as if it were actually killing prey was comical.

His phone vibrated. Jonathan was calling.

"Hey, Bud. What's going on?"

"Brother! Hey, just checking in. How's the holiday season treating you?"

"Eh, aside from the incessant Christmas music everywhere, its going alright . . . I'm currently attempting to wrap presents and failing miserably. My kitten is trying to attack everything I use, and that's not helping."

"Still have the cat, huh? I always pegged you as more of dog guy."

"It's never too late. Hell, I might get one."

They caught up on wedding and holiday plans. He asked about Emilia, and Jonathan divulged that she started dating someone. The news hurt, but he reminded himself that she was entitled to her freedom. Emilia was clear about her intentions to move on, and he wouldn't fault her for it.

After a few minutes, Nate could tell Jonathan was dancing around something.

"Jon? is there anything else you want to talk about?"

Jonathan hesitated. "Nate, why don't you come up north for the holidays? I'd love to host you, and Mom wants to see you . . ."

"I'm not sure, Jon . . . I may not meet her with the same enthusiasm, and I don't want to make the holidays awkward."

"Can you at least call her? She hasn't been in good health lately; it would cheer her up."

"What's wrong?"

"Her blood pressure is out of control; it's now affecting her heart."

Nate felt his anxiety climbing. It had been so long since he let himself feel anything for his mother, much less concern.

"I won't make it for the holidays this year, Bud. But I will call her, okay?"

"That's fine, Big Bro. You can meet Daniela and catch up with Mom at the wedding."

———

The next evening, he sat in his living room by the fireplace, a stiff drink in his hands, and admired the two-foot tree he had placed in the corner. On his way home from a meeting, he had driven past a tree farm where he spotted the small fir. He surprisingly gave in to impulse, something uncommon for him, and brought it home. He found Emilia's holiday décor in the garage and tried to decorate it, but it left a lot to be desired.

It wasn't long before Capri began attacking the ornaments and climbed into the tree. He read online that cats hate the sound of foil and the smell of citrus, so he sprayed the tree with lemon scented furniture polish, and laid foil down all around it.

That did the trick.

The moment Capri set foot on the foil, she jumped three feet in the air and scurried off to her cat tree.

Nate met with his realtor earlier that day to discuss listing the house and finding something smaller, maybe a condo. The home had appreciated significantly since they had it built, and he could live comfortably for some time until he figured out his next career steps.

In that moment, perhaps for the first time, he felt proud of his accomplishments. Even though none of what had transpired in his life had gone as planned, he realized how much his hard work paid off. He was able to provide for himself and Emilia. In that sense, he had succeeded.

The flames in front of him danced, almost tauntingly, reminding him of the feelings he'd worked so hard to suppress. He didn't want to call his mother and lash out, especially now that he'd learned of her health problems.

Ann once told him that the deepest wounds sometimes feel less severe if a cast is built around them. But why automatically treat a wound as a break? Some wounds need air; they need to be brought into the light, so they can finally heal.

When he and Emilia eloped, his mother had called him every name in the book. She accused him of abandoning her and

Jonathan, and called him a coward for not staying to keep them safe. She even accused Emilia of being a whore.

He had cut ties with her then.

Years later, Jonathan had called to inform him that Rick had died in a car accident. When Nate had no reaction, Jonathan called him insensitive. He accused Nate of being bitter and selfish for leaving and tried to downplay what they had gone through. Nate reminded Jonathan that he had also left as soon as he had the chance. That conversation had caused one of Nate's worst spirals and they didn't speak for years. After everything he had done to protect their family, why was he being made to feel like the crazy one for being angry?

The memories stung as they resurfaced, so Nate decided to call her another day, but fate had other plans.

Just then, his phone rang. It was a New York area code.

He took a deep breath, then answered.

"Nathan?" the frail voice asked.

His heart broke. "Yeah, Mom."

Her voice cracked as she told him how much she missed the sound of his voice. "I didn't think I'd ever get to hear your voice again. Jon called me this morning and told me you would call. Excuse me for being forward, but I just couldn't wait anymore. I asked him to give me your number."

"It's okay. How are you feeling?"

She sighed, "I'm old, Nathan. If it's not one thing hurting or broken, it's another."

"I'm beginning to understand," Nate chuckled.

"Nathan, I . . . I need to tell you some things, and I would have much preferred to say them in person, but I don't think Jonathan's wedding is the appropriate place. Are you okay talking over the phone?"

"Yeah, what's on your mind?"

"It feels like as we age, there is an invisible filter in our minds that withers away. I spend a lot of time alone, where I reflect on my life, and I've tried to process everything I—we—went through."

The rolling wave of nausea built in Nate's stomach. While she spoke, he muted himself so he could take deep breaths. He was prepared for a revised version of all the previous accusations pitted against him.

"Nathan, I am so sorry for not protecting you."

Time stopped. He never, *never* expected that.

"I realize now that I was never weak, I was just taught to think that I was. My mother was beaten by my father, my grandmother was beaten by my grandfather, so on and so on. Your father didn't ever lay a finger on me, but he was a womanizer. When he passed, he was found in another woman's bed."

Nate was shocked. He hadn't expected to learn about him this way. It certainly explained why she rarely spoke of him.

She continued, "When Rick came along, he promised to love me and take care of you boys. He lied. I realized a year into the relationship that he was abusive, but violence was all I ever knew, so I stayed. I tried to keep everything in perfect order to avoid his anger and realized too late that we were not the issue, Rick was. As you got older, Nathan, I grew less patient with you, because any misstep could get us in trouble with him. That was not fair to you. You were a child." Her voice broke, "I did not have the emotional strength to face you when you would rightfully confront me. You were right to ask me why we didn't leave the abuse, Hijo. You were right."

Nate's tears had long been flowing. "Mom, try not to get too worked up, it's not good for you," he whispered.

"Well, If I have to die getting this out, I will. You didn't deserve to be treated that way by Rick, or me, Nathan. You deserved better, and I now understand how my behavior affected our relationship. I was also wrong to call you and your wife those horrible things."

Nate felt decades of virulent rage wash away. "Mom, I . . . I accept your apology. It's a lot to process in the moment but know that it means a lot. I spent years being angry at you. I hope we can work our way back to a good place."

"I would love that. I've missed you."

After agreeing to a video chat later that week, Nate hung up and laid back on the floor. He pressed the heel of his cold palms to his eyes to soothe the burn.

He had already decided he needed to forgive his mother and move on for Jonathan's big day, but he never, in a million years, expected such a heartfelt apology from her.

Things were looking up, oh finally . . .

Nate feels wetness beneath his back. When his eyes open, he sees pillowy clouds slowly drifting in a bright blue sky. The air is warm and fresh, and waves crash peacefully against the shore. As he sits up, he surveys the mountains in the distance. They remind him of a tropical mountain range, full of trees from base to peak. Palm trees line the entrance into the woods. The aroma of grilled fruit fills the air.

Off in the distance, someone is walking toward him. A man

appears, and he is carrying what appears to be firewood. He is tall and lean, with a clean-shaven head and big ears.

He approaches with a wide smile. His mouth opens and Nate can tell he is saying "Hi, Nathan," but there is no sound.

"I'm sorry, I can't hear you," Nate says, trying to remember how he got there, "Do you know what this place is?"

The man smiles. *You know where we are.* Nate hears his voice, clear as day, but his lips don't move. That is creepy, but he doesn't feel uncomfortable in the least.

The man points to a tree in the distance. Nate looks over and notices a tree further down the shore. He takes a few steps toward it; it seems out of place and is the only one of its kind on the beach. It hangs over large rocks and its flowers are different colors.

Go there . . . he hears the man say behind his back.

"What's over there?" Nate turns to ask, but the man is gone. Suddenly, the sky turns an ominous shade of gray, and the waves pick up in intensity. Nate slowly backs further inland when he trips on a large rock, falling backward. Except he doesn't land.

He just keeps falling.

9

SQUARE ONE

December was always a bittersweet month. No matter how much I tried to stay lighthearted and festive, something always happened, and my anxiety would trigger.

The stress ensued shortly after the hair trials with Osvaldo. I managed to pull off the styles both brides requested, much to my own surprise. They wanted voluminous hair with lots of braids and curls. They wore tiaras and floor-length veils. Our lunch date after the trial appointment was a lot more fun, and we laughed until the servers began side-eying us for being a little too rambunctious at lunch time.

Osvaldo invited me to a dinner show his partner was starring in, and I told him about Will. Although excited for me, he did make it a point to ask if I was truly ready to move on. "Honey, I won't presume to know what's best for you better than you do. It's just that twenty years is a long time . . . you want to make *sure* you are ready to share yourself with another person, you understand?"

I could tell he came from a place of respect, so I didn't begrudge his advice. "I appreciate you looking out for me, Os," I said as I took his hand, "It means a lot. Besides, Will and I are just dating right now. I am definitely taking things slow."

He patted my hand then sighed. "Listen, you and I worked magic in those hair trials. I have no doubt the wedding will be just as fun. Maybe we can work together on other gigs after the holidays?"

"Yes, absolutely! I can put my job hunt on hold. Between events and helping my sister-in-law plan her wedding, it will keep me busy," I gushed.

Osvaldo eyed me with a sneaky smile. It reminded me of a SpongeBob episode I watched many years ago. "Sister-in-law?" he asked.

"Well, no. I mean my . . . soon-to-be-ex-sister-in-law?" I paused because I wasn't making any sense, "My friend!" I shouted, a little too excitedly.

"I'm just giving you hell, Darlin, I know what you meant."

"Now that I think of it, could I book you to do Daniela's bridal makeup? I was originally going to do hair and makeup as a wedding gift, but I want to her to feel pampered."

"Of course! When is the wedding?"

"First weekend in March."

He scrolled through his phone. "I am open that weekend!"

We agreed to meet at a local coffee shop and ride together to the wedding venue, then parted ways. Two days later, we were fresh faced and ready for action.

Unfortunately, both ceremonies were a disaster.

We didn't realize the twin brides were vicious rivals; they must have been on their best behavior during the hair trials. While bride number one got dressed, bride number two (acting as maid of honor) drank one too many mimosas and got too close to the bride. She tripped and we all watched the mimosa land on the bride's gown in slow motion.

Chaos erupted.

The bridal party shouted back and forth, everyone rushing to find something to dab the stain and get her cleaned up. One bridesmaid stepped on the bride's veil, yanking it out of her hair and sending bobby pins flying everywhere.

Osvaldo's falsetto cries would have been funny any other time, but we were all in damage control mode. I tried to re-pin her hair while she shouted expletives at the maid of honor. Os's look of horror validated my feelings. We were contracted to stay on premises for touch ups throughout the day. As a result, we were invited to attend the reception as guests, and watched the cattiness unfold.

We needed that day to be over.

A couple days later, bride number two was up. One would think they would have learned from their mistakes. But bride number one (now acting as matron of honor) had other plans. Right before the photographer snapped a veil picture, bride number one walked right up to her sister and yanked her veil off, hard.

Chaos erupted again.

It was the sickest déjà vu I'd ever experienced.

We left those events speechless, and Osvaldo promised to give the feedback to his colleague.

"I will never, ever, *ever* work with them again," he swore.

Despite all the horrors I had witnessed at the wedding ceremonies, I got some inspiration for décor that I sent to Daniela.

"The final guest count is sixty," she exclaimed. "We chose a small venue right on the beach."

"Oh, that's great! What's it called?"

"The Venue," she giggled. "It's very close to where you are staying. Do you and Raquel want to come look at it with me?"

The Venue was so close, I could have probably walked. After touring the space, we all had a better idea of Daniela's vision. We spent most of December creating a wedding mood board, and Sage put me in touch with some reputable vendors. Raquel created different table centerpiece options, which all looked fabulous. Daniela chose white and pink roses in a tall crystal beaded trumpet vase. With that, she landed on an ivory, gold, and baby pink theme.

"I want sparkle everywhere!" she declared.

We designed her wedding website and wedding invitations were ordered. Will called a few times but I let it go to voicemail so I could devote my attention to Daniela. When I finally called him back, he seemed put out that I hadn't responded.

"Is everything okay?" I asked.

"Yeah, Honey. Just missed the sound of your voice . . . how was your day?"

"Busy! I've been working on wedding plans with Daniela."

"Who is that again?"

"My brother-in-law's fiancé."

The phone went so quiet, I had to check that we were still connected.

"Your . . . ex-brother-in-law?" Will asked slowly.

"Yes, sorry, that's what I meant. I am the matron of honor and pseudo wedding planner," I joked.

"I see." He sounded distant.

"Will, are you sure you're okay?"

"Yeah, I'm okay. I have another work trip coming up before the holiday break . . . I'd love to see you before I leave."

"I'm free tonight. How about dinner and a movie?"

"Sounds like a plan. I'll pick you up around seven."

I was excited to see Will again. We had gone out a few more times after our steamy tapas date. Those encounters were a little more subdued, and we got to know each other a lot more. He mentioned that he wanted to start a family soon, to which I stayed silent. I didn't feel comfortable mentioning my infertility issues; it was personal, and I wasn't even sure how things with Will would pan out.

Our date night was fun, and after another hot make out session in his car, we agreed to meet up when he returned. I'm not sure what happened while he was away, but his demeanor changed again. He was still gentle and respectful, but I could tell he was being more guarded.

I was excited about the upcoming holidays, but when they arrived, everything seemed dull.

I spent Noche Buena with mom and Raquel, then Christmas day with Jonathan and Daniela. There, I briefly reunited with Nate and Jonathan's mom, Gloria. I had only interacted with her twice before, once as a kid when she caught me sneaking into Nate's bedroom, then when Nate moved out and she told him he made a mistake in marrying me.

She was surprisingly cordial, friendly even, but wasn't feeling well so Jonathan took her home.

Everyone around me had a great time. They caroled and laughed, ate and drank, and enjoyed the gifts I bought them.

But I was in a fog.

I would smile when appropriate, laugh at the jokes, even carol along with them. But inside, I felt disconnected with everything. There was a pressure building inside me; something constantly pulled at my thoughts, not allowing me to enjoy the moment with family and friends.

I even felt that way at Andy's Kwanzaa celebration. The last time I gathered with these same people, I was overjoyed; I bonded with everyone, and we had a blast. This time, I felt like the odd one out. I could tell by Andy's smile that Will told her about us. He held my hand and kept me close, but I knew something was off. When I asked about it, he brushed it off and said he was tired, or that work was draining him.

That night, as he walked me to my car, I felt his distance growing.

"Shoot straight with me, Will," I said gently, "Are you not interested in me anymore?"

He looked surprised at my question. "What? Of course, I'm interested in you."

"I sense that something is off with you, but when I ask, you say it's nothing. It's only been a month since we've starting dating, and I feel like you may be shutting down on me."

He stared intently at me, as if trying to solve a riddle. Then, he said something unexpected. "I don't like liars."

My shock and confusion didn't seem to faze him.

He continued. "I'm not calling you a liar, Honey. I'm saying that, in general, I don't like liars. You asked me about my previous relationship, but I wasn't comfortable sharing details, because it was a painful break up, and you and I are so new. But leading with dishonesty would be hypocritical, and I've been debating whether I should open up about it."

"You could have just said that, Will. I would've respected your space and trusted you'd tell me when you felt comfortable."

"I realize that, now. I've also come to the realization that I may have developed some trust issues." He sighed, "My ex and I were solid, at least I thought so. She told me she wanted marriage and kids. I did too. I've always wanted to be a father. We were together for three years when I purchased an engagement ring. Before I had the chance to pop the question, I found out she had cheated."

My eyes widened. Will was such a catch. I couldn't fathom someone stepping out on him.

"I know," he nodded. "Shocked me too. I thought she was happy. I tried to be as attentive as possible, Andy taught me to be an open communicator. We weren't going through a rough patch or anything, it just . . . happened. She said it was because she was scared of commitment, that I was wholesome, and she felt she didn't deserve that, yada yada. Anyway, I bought it and forgave her."

I suspected by his tone, that wasn't the deal breaker.

"I began to notice her body changing. She wasn't eating as much, and she was getting dizzy spells. Shortly after, we found out she was pregnant. She was thrilled! After a couple of months, we had an official baby announcement and everything. Then, she miscarried."

I felt a familiar gut punch. "I'm sorry, Will," I said softly, averting my eyes.

"I was devastated, but she seemed fine, like, absolutely fine. That concerned me, as I didn't want her to suppress something like that. I tried to encourage her to seek help or talk to me about her feelings, but she said that she accepted it wasn't the right time. Instead, she became insistent on us getting married. One day, I was opening the mail and noticed she left some paperwork on the counter. It was from a nearby women's health clinic, not her primary care physician. I didn't question her on it and went about my business."

"A few weeks later, I took her mother out to lunch. I wanted ideas for an engagement surprise and thought it would be cool to include her in the plans."

So thoughtful, I thought.

"What I thought was going to be a joyous occasion, turned into a nightmare. Her mother was feeling tremendous guilt about the fact that her daughter lied to me. I was told that she didn't miscarry. She terminated the pregnancy."

My hand flew to my mouth. Will's expressive eyes dimmed as he relived the painful experience.

"The news that she terminated, although devastating, wasn't what crushed me. It's her body, Emilia. I would have respected her wishes if she wasn't ready. It was the elaborate lie that infuriated me. When I confronted her, she wasn't remorseful about lying at all. The cherry on top? She told me that I shouldn't mourn so much, that she had been unfaithful again, and wasn't sure who the father was, which had fueled her decision to terminate."

I was in disbelief. That woman was so callous in her delivery, and I could see it deeply wounded him. I hugged him as tight as I could and felt his stiff body relaxing.

"Thank you for sharing. I'm sorry you had to go through that."

"She was right about one thing. It wasn't the right time. And she wasn't the right one."

He smiled at me with his warm eyes. I tried to smile back, then hugged him again.

Truth was, I wasn't sure I was the right one, either.

New Year's Eve was quiet. Sage and I made dinner, went to the Bluff to get some air, then talked a little bit before bed.

"I'm surprised you and Will aren't out and about," she teased, wagging her brows.

"He asked, but I haven't been feeling myself lately, and wasn't in the mood for crowds."

"Are you okay?" she asked as she rubbed my arm. Her hands were silky and smooth.

My first reaction was to downplay my anxiety spells, but something in my gut told me she might be able to help.

"Sage, do you dream?"

"All day every day!" she gleefully responded.

I chuckled, "I mean, do you dream in your sleep?"

"Yes, I have lucid dreams from time to time."

"What do they mean?"

"That's entirely individual, my dear. Most religions believe it is communication between God and Conscience. Other practices believe it is our higher self taking a break from the body and hanging out in the cosmos. Science is still learning about it, but recognizes dreaming as a state of consciousness, in which the brain is actively trying to process a thought, memory, or trauma."

I nodded, trying to figure out what the hell *my* dreams signified. "When my father passed away, I began dreaming of him regularly. When I moved in with you, the dreams stopped."

"Change of scenery perhaps?" Sage pondered.

"I thought so too. I chalked it up to being around my sister and his side of the family. But lately, I am dreaming of him again, and it's keeping me up at night."

Sage nodded, "There could be many reasons for that, Emi. I don't want to speculate whether there is a spiritual or psychological reason, but I do suggest journaling and meditation before going to bed tonight. Maybe clearing your mind will allow you to rest."

"I will try that." I smiled.

Just then, Sage's phone vibrated, signaling the start of the new year. "Happy Gregorian New Year, Emilia!" she cheered as she embraced me.

I laughed and hugged my friend back, then headed to my room.

I pulled out the journal I'd purchased at Emory's bookstore when I first arrived and chastised myself for not following through with my goal of journaling. I probably would have already been better if I had started back then. Not knowing where to begin, I jotted down a few random words. After some time, I was pouring my heart out onto the pages.

I reminded myself that the dreams about my dad were just my mind's way of coping with being around Raquel, my mom, and my grandmother again, and I shouldn't stress about it. After some stretches, I put on a few guided meditations and gave it a whirl.

My mind raced on about trivial things, and I just couldn't turn it off. I finally gave up around three a.m. and climbed into bed. The last I remember is counting sheep and repeating *New Year, New Me* to myself until I fell asleep.

A few weeks later, the new year was in full swing, and I felt as if nothing had changed.

While everyone was flocking to the gym or scouting out new therapists, I didn't even bother setting a new year's resolution. My internal clock had flipped for some reason, and it seemed that nighttime signaled my brain to go into turbo mode.

I'd be lying in bed, just about to doze off when my brain would decide it needed a to-do list for the following day or it simply couldn't rest. As much as I tried ignoring it, there was no relief unless I wrote the list down. Sometimes, I'd wake up thinking I heard a neighbor driving past the house with the bass cranked up, only to realize it was the sound of my heart beating out of my chest.

I became obsessed with watching the local news just in case someone I knew was on it, and I was constantly checking up on everyone. When they asked if I was okay, I'd make up the excuse that I missed them, but really, I just needed to make sure everyone was still alive.

I tried to mask my anxiety with Sage, but she was smarter than that. Whenever we hung out, she made sure we were doing something relaxing, so I'd drift off. I never remembered my dreams when I was in her presence.

Everything around me was fine, but everything inside me felt like it could combust in a moment's notice. Even Will's sunny disposition returned. He said he felt as if a huge weight had lifted off his chest when he told me about his ex. Meanwhile, I felt my chest compress every time I saw him, because I had yet to mention my infertility issues.

It's not that I owed him an explanation, but I could tell he was interested in something serious with me, and I didn't want something as important as having children—or my inability to have them—to be perceived as an afterthought once he was emotionally invested.

Another issue was, I wasn't sure *I* was emotionally invested. As wonderful and attractive as he was, there was an emotional block there for me, and I couldn't figure out why.

With Sage out of the country visiting her grandparents and Will on an extended business trip, I spent my days in bed trying to catch up on sleep and my nights nursing my increasing panic attacks.

One night, I got the bright idea to sneak onto the beach and hang out at the hidey spot. The sound of the waves helped slow down the thoughts enough to make me tired again. On one of my strolls, I decided to keep walking along the shore until the cove ended, and I discovered that The Venue, where Daniela and Jonathan, were getting married was just past the trees.

When I made it back to the car, I felt like I'd run a marathon. Excited to get some sleep, I headed back to the house, took a shower, and headed for bed.

This is the present day.

I have never stepped foot in my grandmother's house as an adult, so I am aware that this is a dream.

Everything in the house is eerily dark and quiet, except for the hallway light that is on and the sound of a wall clock ticking. I look over to the kitchen and notice a figure sitting in a chair at the dining table, staring out the window. I can't make out who it is, and an uneasy feeling grows in my stomach.

"Who's there?" I ask, still sitting on the couch and feeling no sensation in my legs.

"Shhh . . ." the figure says. The voice sounds hollow.

"Who are you?" I whisper.

The figure turns its head to me, then steadily rises. The ticking is gradually getting louder and there is a deafening bass filling the room.

"Shhhh . . ." the figure repeats as it approaches.

I see a woman's silhouette begin to form.

As I open my mouth to scream for help, the woman rushes toward me at a frightening speed. She appears right in front of me, and bends until she is eye level with me.

My blood runs cold as I realize who it is. Marta's swollen and bruised face is now partially illuminated by the hallway light.

"Shhh," she whispers. "When he walks through that door, stay quiet, and don't let her cry. . ."

Tears run down my face as I open my mouth to scream. She covers my mouth and all I can smell is decay.

"Emiliaaah . . ." she sings. The sound of her vacant drawl fills me with dread, "You know what will happen if you make a sound, don't you?"

I nod slowly.

She straightens and looks at me for a moment, then methodically turns and walks toward the hallway, one step at a time, in tandem with the ticking clock. When she reaches the door, it flies open. I hear my father's name and her blood curdling scream.

My blood curdling scream.

10

PLEDGE YOUR TROTH

"Will broke up with you on Valentine's Day?" Raquel shouted into the phone.

"Flaca, there's no need to yell. And I wouldn't call it a breakup . . . We were never an official couple. We were dating, and after a rather difficult conversation, decided it was best not to continue." I slapped my legs again hoping they would stop tingling. My body ached all over.

I needed rest.

"Okay, you need to spill. What happened? Everything was going so well."

I was sick and tired of having to explain myself to everyone. I was accustomed to facing my troubles alone. No one was ever this interested when Nate and I had problems.

Why the sudden interest?

I tried to hide my irritation and filled her in. "During the holidays, he told me about his previous relationship. His ex-girlfriend cheated on him, then terminated a pregnancy he thought they were both really excited about. He later found out the reason why; she cheated on him a second time and suspected the pregnancy was a result of that affair."

"Oh my God. Poor Will . . . But what does that have to do with the breakup?"

"Don't interrupt," I huffed.

"Okay, sheesh."

"Will really wants children. I felt like I was being dishonest by not telling him about my infertility issues. Finally, I opened up about it. He asked if I was open to adoption, and I asserted that I didn't want to pursue children if not biologically. At first, he seemed to accept my answer, but as the weeks passed, I noticed him becoming more withdrawn." I sighed, "After an awkward Valentine's date, I confronted him, and he admitted that he didn't think this would work long term."

"I'm sorry, Emi," she groaned.

"It's okay. I'm glad he ended things now. I wouldn't want him to resent me for it later."

Been there, done that.

"Well, if you need anything, let me know. You can talk to me, Sis. I've noticed you're also a little withdrawn . . ."

"All I need from you, is to be here on time tomorrow so we can do your hair and makeup trial. I know how picky you are."

"Relax, Sister. We're still a week away from the wedding."

"That's not a lot of time. I need you and Mom squared away, so we can pay full attention to Daniela."

"Roger that," she sighed.

After hanging up, I decided to run a bath.

I desperately missed Sage's company. She had to stay with her grandparents longer than expected. Her grandmother had not previously mentioned that her cancer returned, and although her grandfather was in good health, managing everything in the home was too much work for him alone. Sage was making sure she was receiving adequate medical care and wanted to hire some domestic help. She called to let me know she was extending her trip a few more weeks and caught on to my exhaustion.

That intuitive mind of hers was impressive.

"I may look into a therapist or something," I replied as I blew some of the bath suds away from me.

"Does this have to do with you and Will?" she asked cautiously.

"No, I'm handling that pretty well. I realize it seems a bit unusual, but I also feel that Will and I are better off as friends. My main concern is that I haven't been sleeping."

"Are you still dreaming of your father?"

"Yes. I'm able to sleep a little during the day. I average about three to four hours, but something flips at night; I can't seem to turn my brain off."

"What are you doing at night to try to calm your mind?"

"At first I meditated and journaled as you suggested, then I tried yoga, teas, aromatherapy, white noise, grey noise, purple noise, no noise!" I snickered, "Nothing is working." I hesitated before admitting, "I've also been going to the hidey spot at night . . . It is so peaceful; I hang out there until I feel I can't stay awake any longer."

Sage chuckled. "That beach is magical, but please be safe out there! We've never seen anyone else at the cove, but you never know. Also, if you don't feel comfortable talking about your anxiety with someone you know, I completely understand, but promise me you'll at least talk to someone? Sleep deprivation can torment an anxious mind."

I agreed.

"How do you feel about seeing Nate?" she asked.

"Indifferent. The rehearsal dinner should be interesting. I hope that he doesn't make things awkward. As long as he doesn't insist on rehashing things, we'll be okay."

The next day, I called all the vendors to reconfirm head counts and finalize balances. I coordinated with the photographer and videographer. I had learned early on in the process that Daniela loved the fun part of planning, but not the logistics.

When I stopped by their house to drop off the table centerpieces, Jonathan told me that Nate was in town, then paused for a reaction. Jonathan's boyish expressions were always cute.

"That's good, Jon. I'm glad he made it safe."

"Yeah, he's with my mom right now."

That gave me pause. "Is he . . . Is everything okay?"

"Yeah, I think they are starting to work through some things."

"Wow. That's great!"

Jonathan nodded knowingly. I guess he had a similar reaction. "Just brace yourself, Sis. He's not the man you last saw in North Carolina."

It was my turn to chuckle. "Ok, Jon. Thanks for the heads up."

I drove away wondering what he meant by that.

I had Raquel and my mom come over together for their trials and made a mental note to never do that again.

Aside from not sitting still, they both wanted another detailed account of my breakup with Will, kept changing their minds about eye shadow colors, and Raquel could not decide on a hairstyle.

I was hardly making any progress because Raquel kept turning around to talk to my mom. Exasperated, I grabbed Raquel's cheeks between my fingers. "Flaca. Stop. Moving."

"Eva, do something. She's being a jerk . . ." she complained.

My mom had already been eyeing me, but that wasn't a surprise. I always felt like she was looking for something about me to judge.

"Hija, you look run down," she said flatly.

"Thanks, Mom. Appreciate that."

"You know I don't mean it like that. You look tired and you've lost weight."

"I know. I haven't been sleeping lately."

"You've always been a weird sleeper, but you've never lost weight because of it."

I ignored her observation and focused on blending Raquel's eyeshadow. Once Raquel was satisfied with her makeup look, I sat my mom down. Instead of pulling out her phone and searching for an inspiration pic, she brought out a 1996 issue of Vanidades.

"Mom, have you really been saving this magazine all this time?"

"Yeah! I used to collect trinkets, but magazines were cheaper. I like to keep them in sleeves; they could be worth a lot of money one day!"

I didn't remember ever seeing her trinket collection but didn't press further. She wanted a 90s bombshell updo, which wouldn't require much effort since she already had thick brown hair and sported bangs.

Raquel chose a waterfall braid and loose curls.

When I was finished, I admired my work. "Don't you two look smashing," I mused. "Did you pick up the dresses?"

"Yes! They're in the car, I'll go get them," Raquel said as she ran past me.

"Emilia," my mom called.

"¿Mande?" I muttered as I put the hair tools away.

"Look at me."

The look on her face told me there was no point in masking around her. She would poke and poke until I spilled.

I sighed loudly. "I've been dreaming about Pablo nonstop for a month. The nightmares are getting worse, and I'm beyond exhausted. Please stop pushing the issue in front of Raquel."

"Don't call him Pablo. He's your father."

I heard myself suck my teeth before I realized what I was doing. That was considered a battle cry when I was a kid.

My mom's wide-eyed glare confirmed she was thinking the same thing.

"I'm sorry. I just don't have this veneration for him like everyone around me seems to."

"Seems to what?" Raquel asked as she walked in with our garment bags.

"Nothing," I muttered.

Raquel stripped down to her undies in record time to try on the dress.

Daniela had picked up on everyone's anxiety at having to choose a dress, so she decided. The bridal party would wear a knee length cocktail dress with sparkly sequins shaped in geometric patterns. She chose champagne gold for Raquel and her cousin and a blush pink for me as her matron of honor. The dress made Raquel's skin tone pop.

"You look stunning, Flaca!"

"Now you can find a husband," my mom hollered from the bathroom.

"Ma," I chastised.

"Oh, stop it! I can't say anything around you. Besides," she said as she walked back in, "I may just one up you ladies in this number." She twirled around in a beige, floor-length, cape sleeve gown, also lined with sparkly sequins, also of Daniela's choosing.

"Look at you!" Raquel and I exclaimed in unison.

"I thought the beige would wash you out, but you picked a great color, Mami."

"When I tried it on, I felt fabulous. Gloria's gown is the same color, but a different style."

"You went shopping with Gloria?" I asked, perplexed.

"Yes, Daniela took me and Gloria shopping a few weeks ago. She was very nice, but her health is failing."

"What's wrong with her?"

"Her blood pressure, Mija."

"I see."

I wondered how Nate was dealing with their reunion.

The Venue was a one-stop shop for all the wedding activities. Inside, there was a fine dining restaurant, used to host cocktail hours and rehearsal dinners. This was convenient as a wedding party could hop to the event rooms for rehearsals with ease.

I had not gotten to bed until seven a.m. that morning, then had to be up at ten a.m. to meet the girls at the salon for mani-pedis.

I was running on fumes.

"Where is Gloria?" I asked Daniela while I relished the massage chair's knead setting.

"She had a doctor's appointment this morning, so she got her nails done yesterday."

"Gotcha." Everyone sounded so concerned when I asked about Gloria. I wondered if her condition was more serious than they let on. Those thoughts quickly washed away when my foot massage began. I entered another dimension when Lucy, the pedicurist, ran her hands down my calves.

After the nail appointment, I stopped by the bakery to finalize payment, then headed back to the florist to review a slight bouquet change, before running across town to grab some favors for the evening. Raquel took it upon herself to decorate for the rehearsal dinner and recruited Daniela's cousin, much to my relief.

My dizzy spells were becoming more frequent, due to exhaustion, and I was forgetting to eat and drink. My legs were always tingling; it felt like ants were crawling up my thighs, and I was helpless to stop it.

To add to my discomfort, Will sent a long text message expressing his regret for calling things off on Valentine's Day. He reiterated that although he felt it was the right thing to do, I was "an amazing girl" and he hoped we could remain friends.

He signed off by writing, "*You deserve the world, Emilia.*"

Too bad "the world" doesn't agree.

I kept my response short and sweet:

Will, I appreciate the kind words, but they really aren't necessary. I understand and accept your decision and will always consider you a friend. I'll see you around, okay? <3

As I walked into the closet to grab my outfit, I stared longingly at my bed.

I had a few hours until the event, so I tried to squeeze in a nap. I laid on Sage's plush pillows and let out a deep sigh as I felt my lids grow heavy.

When I came to, I reached for my phone in a panic thinking I had overslept.

I had only slept for ten minutes.

I threw my arms over my eyes. "Ugh, I give up!" I screamed as I stomped to the bathroom and slammed the door.

―――――――――

As I pulled into The Venue, my stomach began to leap. It wasn't butterflies; I was anxious.

Anxious about being in a room with Nate and my family again. That had not happened in over twenty years, so their reactions were unpredictable.

It was still nippy in early March, so I wore a chunky tunic with a turtleneck, black knit tights, and booties. I paired it with my faithful sherpa coat and let my long, tousled hair loose. My makeup was evening-appropriate—with a little extra concealer for the dark circles under my eyes—and I threw on a pair of earrings Raquel had given me for Christmas.

When I arrived at cocktail hour, I noticed several wedding parties were present, all talking and laughing. I was relieved. I expected one of those movie scenes where I walked in, and everyone went silent.

Egotistical much, Emilia?

Raquel and my mom walked over to me, and Raquel slipped her arm in mine. "I'm not letting you go tonight, okay, Emi?"

I was grateful for her support; I hated awkward encounters. Her intentions were noble, but the bride and groom had other plans. I looked around at our small party. We were eight total, plus the mothers and the officiant.

Except there were two missing: Nate and Gloria.

My panic slowly crept up. What if Nate flaked? How was Jonathan going to deal with that?

Just then, Daniela and Jonathan walked in, hand in hand, and we all smiled and applauded. Jonathan's friend Darius, one of the groomsmen, clearly liked to party and was hollering as if we weren't in a room with other people. Jonathan seemed to be in good spirits, so hopefully Nate was bound to show up . . .

I was introduced to the other groomsman, the cousin's brother. Daniela's relatives were timid, and I sensed they felt out of their element. I handed the party favors to the hostess to put at the dinner table, and by the time I got back to the group, my lovely, adoring, all-knowing sister had a cocktail waiting for me.

"Jon, where are Nate and your mom?" I asked while sipping my drink, trying to sound as casual as possible.

"Mom fell behind, so Nate is bringing her," Jon said before tapping his glass, "Guys, a slight change of plans. One of the wedding parties was running behind schedule so we are going to have dinner first, so they can rehearse in the chapel."

After another cocktail and some of the funniest dad jokes Darius could muster, the hostess ushered us over to the private dining area. There, I saw place cards on each plate. Raquel and I noticed we were split up.

I was to sit in between my mother, and Nate.

Before I could process any further, I heard the man himself behind me. "Allow me," he said gently, as he pulled out a chair for both me and my mom.

My "thank you" barely came out as a whisper when I saw him.

Jonathan was not kidding. The man sitting down beside me, was not the Nathan I had left in North Carolina. His wavy hair was tamed into a gentleman's cut. His beard was full and sprinkled with silver, his tan skin looked radiant, and his eyes were lively. He must have kept up with the gym because his sweater and jeans could not hide his bulging muscles.

He was gorgeous, and best of all, he looked happy.

I felt an overwhelming sadness enter my being. He looked like he found something I've desperately searched for since I came back.

I was happy for him, but I was sad for me.

Gloria sat directly across from my mom, next to Jonathan. Every time our eyes met, she would offer me a soft smile, which I'd return, but I was terribly confused. I thought she hated me. Maybe she was happy that Nate and I had broken up?

I felt my mom's hand softly pat my knee. I bet she could sense my anxiety. Nate made conversation with everyone at the table, and although he wasn't ignoring me, he wasn't speaking directly to me, either.

Finally, while we were waiting on the main entrée, he turned to me. "How have you been, Emilia?" he asked.

Emilia? Since when did he call me Emilia?

"I've been good, Nathan. Just adjusting to these winters again," I muttered with a soft smile.

"I hear ya. I brought my kitten with me, and she won't come out from under her blanket unless it's to fight with Oliver."

"She kicks his ass too, Em," Jonathan chimed in.

"You adopted a cat?" *Who was this guy?*

He shrugged. "She more or less adopted me."

Just then, the server came with our entrees. I had ordered the chicken piccata and quickly realized I had no desire to eat. I looked over to Raquel and noticed she and Darius having a grand old time cracking jokes. My mom had ordered the same as me and grimaced at her food.

"Mami, stop making faces at the food," I whispered. She never ventured much outside Hispanic cuisine.

Nate and Jonathan had ordered a surf and turf and were eating like it was their first meal of the day.

Daniela laughed and patted her fiancé's back. "Slow down baby, the food's not going anywhere."

"Nate took me to the gym with him today," Jonathan declared between bites. "I thought it was going to be a regular, full body workout. I haven't exercised so hard since basic training!"

I smiled and nodded, trying not to make it obvious that I was checking out Nate's biceps.

After dinner, the coordinator escorted us to the chapel to begin our rehearsal. Everyone was loose and relaxed. Everyone, except me. I wanted this to be perfect for Daniela and found myself annoyed that the groomsmen kept goofing off.

"Fix your face, Emi," Raquel said as she slipped her arm in mine, "you're giving everyone the stink eye."

I closed my eyes. "I know. I'm sorry. I'm just cranky."

"Well, when you get home tonight, have a couple of glasses of wine. That's what I've been doing lately."

"Are you still not sleeping?"

"It has gotten better, but I have my days. Just don't make the wine a habit," she ordered.

The officiant cleared his throat. "Gather around everyone. We will begin our run through of Daniela and Jonathan's ceremony. Please keep in mind that a videographer will be filming and there will also be a live stream of the event for Daniela's family."

After a laundry list of instructions, we were ready to begin. The chapel was beautiful and bright with a wide aisle. Jonathan would walk down the aisle with both my mom and Gloria on his arms, followed by Nate and myself, Raquel and Darius, Daniela's cousin and her brother, and finally, Daniela, in all her glory.

As we lined up, I noticed another difference about Nate. He stood taller, with more confidence. He was five-nine but looked a foot taller.

When it was our turn to walk in, he extended his arm to me. "Shall we?"

I looked up and saw someone I had thought was gone forever. That warm, boyish smirk of his had returned, and all I wanted was to hug him and tell him how much I'd missed him.

It felt as if my best friend had returned.

I grabbed his arm and smiled, my eyes no doubt failing to hide my pain. "Aye, Lord Nathan," I breathed.

Nate laid in bed, lazily rubbing Capri's head while he stared up at the ceiling. Being back on Long Island after so many years brought on so many complex emotions, but he was proud of his ability to process them and not feel like he was headed for a spiral.

Being with his mom the past few days was like a balm to the soul. She was nurturing with him, and she allowed him to treat her the same; that was something he hadn't known he needed. Although her health was worrisome, she was on the mend. Her biggest hurdle was learning to listen to her body when it was tired. That morning, he arrived early to take her to a doctor's appointment, and she had spent hours in the kitchen preparing a breakfast feast.

Meeting Daniela and seeing how happy she made Jonathan, was the icing on the cake. Daniela was a small but mighty woman. She came from a hard-working upbringing, and she was fiercely proud of her culture, one that he and Jonathan shared and looked forward to exploring.

He had come to Long Island with the intention of leaving as quickly as he came, but for the first time ever, it felt like a home he sorely missed. It wasn't the place. It was the people. His mom, his brother . . . his wife. *They* were his home.

Nate thought he could be cordial, but the moment he saw Emilia, every memory, every emotion, came rushing back. She was as beautiful as ever, her hair long like she had worn it all those years ago. He was a tad concerned about her weight; she was thinner than when she moved out. Regardless, his heart skipped for her, and although he masked it well, he wasn't sure how much longer he could hide it. He wanted his best friend back, and he wasn't leaving without giving it one more try.

11

HERE COMES THE BRIDE

June 2005

"Amor!" he exclaimed.

I was both surprised and annoyed at his phone call. Surprised, because he hadn't called to wish me a happy birthday in years. Annoyed, because I didn't know how he had gotten my phone number, and my grief-stricken brain hadn't thought to check the caller ID before answering.

"Hey, Papi," I answered. "How you been?"

"Oh, you know, working on some side projects here and there." His words were slurred, but I had no doubt he was at work, drunk. "How are you?"

"I'm good," I lied.

I wasn't in the mood to talk about the miscarriage, much less with him. And despite Nate's attempts to cheer me up, I refused to celebrate my birthday.

It felt blasphemous; my babies would never get a birthday.

"Listen, Hija, I'm calling because, I've run into some problems.

Marta has been a little irresponsible with the money coming in, and I was wondering if you could lend me some?"

Lies.

Not only was Marta frugal with money, but Raquel had filled me in on their recent break up. Marta kicked him out after he put her head through a wall. He was back to using, and his drug habit was way beyond his means.

"I don't have any money."

"You don't even know what it's for," he griped.

"Doesn't change the fact that I don't have it."

He sighed, "Fine. Everything been good?"

"Yes."

"Listen, I got another call coming in . . . I'll call you later." He hung up.

Thanks for the birthday wish, Dad.

It was the big day, and I sorely wished I didn't feel so sick. My stomach had been turning all evening, and I never actually went to bed.

After an early morning soak, I took some acid reducer and a few pain pills for the headache. The wedding coordinator had agreed to let Osvaldo and I arrive an hour before everyone else to set up our beauty stations. I had just finished curling my hair and putting them in rollers when he walked in.

"Emilia, darlin, you are very pale. Are you okay?" he asked, clearly taken aback.

My reflection was a little frightening. I looked gaunt. "I didn't get much sleep last night," I replied.

I didn't even go to sleep last night.

He offered to do my makeup before the rest of the wedding party arrived, and I happily agreed.

"Don't worry, Darlin, your dark circles are no match for my skill," he declared as he dabbed another layer of concealer under my eyes.

"Thank you for offering to do this, Os. I'll gladly compensate you."

"Don't piss me off so early in the morning, Emilia. I don't want your money. I am your friend."

I smiled and fought the tears that wanted to gush out. He would kill me if I ruined the makeup.

Daniela walked in with that familiar bridal glow. Before the hustle and bustle began, she asked us to huddle for a quick word.

"Although I wish my family could be here today, you all have gone above and beyond for me, and made this process memorable. There aren't enough words to express how grateful I am to each of you. I am honored to share my special day with such amazing women . . . and you, Emilia, are already the best sister-in-law anyone could ask for."

The ladies applauded as I embraced Daniela.

As she walked over to my beauty station, Osvaldo brushed past me, that sneaky smile on his face again. "Sister-in-law?" he whispered.

"Shut up," I quipped, unable to hide my smile.

The mood was bright. Everyone was laughing and excited to get dolled up. Raquel assisted Daniela's cousin with her makeup, while my mom steamed everyone's dresses. She was hyper focused on getting every last crease out of Daniela's wedding gown.

Daniela's playlist was great. She had a little bit of everything;

Vicente Fernández, Janet Jackson, Karol G, Rocio Dúrcal, and Madonna. Even I mustered up the energy to sing along. I placed big rollers in her hair so the curls would set while Osvaldo applied her makeup.

"Os, before you begin, I have a little gift for Daniela."

"What's this?" Daniela asked as she opened the envelope I handed her.

"Your new lawyer's contact information. Stefany is one of the best immigration attorneys on the island. I've covered her retainer fee. She can file your petition for permanent residency and push the visa applications for your family."

I held her as she broke into sobs, and Osvaldo mouthed a thank you for making her cry *before* he began her makeup.

While he worked on her, I was able to get through Raquel's glam.

"Where is Gloria?" I asked out loud.

"Jonathan took her to the salon to get her hair and makeup done," Daniela replied, "she is taking pictures with the groomsmen."

"I could have done her hair," I muttered.

Daniela shrugged. Jonathan probably didn't feel comfortable asking me to do it. I don't blame him. I never pursued a relationship with her. It had always felt like a betrayal to Nate.

After getting my mom dolled up, I let Daniela's hair down and pinned one side with a pearl bridal comb. My mom helped her step into her wedding gown while I got dressed and quickly pinned my hair into a loose French twist.

Her something new was a tennis bracelet Gloria had gifted her. Her something borrowed was a pair of antique, natural pearl earrings my mom wore for her wedding. Her something blue was a lacy floral garter adorned with ivory pearls. The photographer snapped away as I buttoned her gown. The moment I clipped her veil into place, she transformed.

Her beauty was captivating.

"You look incredible, Mija," my mom announced. "Jonathan is a very lucky man."

We all rushed to the bride to dab her tears.

"Why aren't you wearing your dress blues?" Nate asked.

"I didn't fit into them," Jonathan bashfully admitted.

Suddenly, Nate heard a thud behind him and spun around. He cackled as he watched Oliver lay his entire body on Jonathan's chest.

"Get up, man. Your tux is going to wrinkle." Nate tried to pull Oliver off, but he wouldn't let up until he finished licking Jonathan's fingers.

Oliver had an important role to play in the nuptials, as he was the ring bearer, but he refused to cooperate. During rehearsal, they had tried to get Oliver to walk down the aisle, but he would not move.

Jonathan hoped Oliver could be persuaded with a drumstick, so he tested his theory. Instead, Oliver tackled him to the ground and stole the drumstick out of his hand.

"He's not going to make it down the aisle, Bud."

"I see that . . ." Jonathan smiled as he patted Oliver's head, "You might just have to pass me the rings."

Nate shook his head. "Where's Mom?"

"She's almost done getting dressed."

"Why did she ask the guys to head to the chapel ahead of us?"

"Mom wanted to speak to us privately before the ceremony."

Nate hoped everything was okay. As she walked into the living room, she stuck her fingers between her teeth and whistled.

"Oliver, ven." she commanded.

He immediately stood and walked to her side, then laid at her feet.

Jonathan and Nate eyed each other in disbelief.

"What?" She smiled, "I raised two boys. I know how to command attention. Now come, sit with me. I want to say a few things before the day begins."

Oliver also walked over to the couch and sat directly in front of her, ready to listen to what she had to say.

"Jonathan, from the moment Nathan saw you, he thought you were his. He wanted to do everything for you—change your diapers, feed you, teach you how to talk."

"Aww, you wuved your wittle brother?" Jonathan teased as he pinched Nate's cheek.

"Yeah, too bad you never got the talking down," Nate smirked.

"When I brought that bastard into our lives," she continued, "your brotherhood became one of survival. I've apologized to you individually, but I wanted to say these things to you together. Learn to enjoy your brotherhood again, boys. Lean on each other, confide in each other. *Be there* for each other. When my time comes to rest, I want to be at peace knowing you two have each other's back."

They each took their mother's hand. "Don't worry about us, Mom. Now that Nate is back, I'm not letting him go anywhere."

Jonathan held back tears. Nate rarely saw him get emotional.

He also reassured her that they would not allow themselves to grow apart again.

They meant it too. Nate had finally gotten the opportunity to express the hurt he was carrying about his trauma not being taken seriously. Jonathan acknowledged that and apologized. He said he had perfected the art of denial, which is why he tried to downplay the shit show they grew up in. To accept Nate's narrative, would mean accepting it had happened to him, too.

Their mom cleared her throat. "Now, about the girls. I need you two need to remember this. You saw, firsthand, what hierarchy can do in a relationship. Listen to your partners, be respectful, and protect them. Do not let your pride and ego trick you into believing they have to put up with your shit. Nathan, Emilia will work her way back to you. I can see it in her eyes, Mijo. She may not realize it, but you two are far from over."

Jonathan nodded in agreement. "She told me she stopped seeing that dude."

Nate nodded, careful not to show his excitement.

"Jonathan," she added, "begin on a solid foundation. Daniela is such a special girl. Expect her to change. Everyone changes, as they should. Give her space to be herself. She will make an excellent wife; not a perfect one. You won't be a perfect husband either. The point is that you try."

She dried her tears and kissed them on the forehead. Nate and Jonathan each wiped their own tears.

Nate never expected a family reunion like this.

She clapped her hands together and stood. "Now, let's party. Oliver! Vámonos."

Oliver walked right alongside his grandma.

We had unseasonably warm weather that morning. Daniela had picked matching, faux fur, mini shawls for us in case it was too cold, but we were already sweating.

"The guys are here," Raquel squealed.

The photographer had us gather in the front lobby to wait for the groomsmen.

"Are they doing a first look?" Raquel whispered in my ear.

"Nope. She wants to see his reaction at the altar," I said.

The event coordinator let us know the guests were entering the chapel through a side entrance and we would walk through the double doors. Jonathan walked in with his mom on his arm, followed by his groomsmen, and finally Nate and Oliver, who was wearing a dog tuxedo.

As soon as Nate saw me, his face changed. His emotions were on full display. I couldn't even try to hide my reaction. He looked amazing, and I smiled back at him.

I'm in trouble.

The coordinator announced, "let's go ahead and get lined up. We are going to get started in just a few minutes. Emilia, the bride wants to speak to you for a moment."

I hurried to the side room where she was waiting and found Osvaldo doing last minute touch ups.

"Emilia, how does he look?" she asked, trying to slow her breathing.

"He looks ready. He walked in looking like a million bucks," I said as I rubbed her hands.

"I'm so nervous. My train is so long, what if I trip?"

"Don't worry. The coordinator will adjust your train and veil, just like we rehearsed. You, keep your eyes on the man you love. It's just you and him in that moment." My voice broke, and I looked up at Osvaldo, who was staring at me intently, holding back his own tears. He didn't need to say anything.

I knew that he knew, my tears were for them. And for Nate.

"Okay," she breathed. "I'm ready."

I kissed her hand, then ran back out with the rest of the party.

When I reached Nate, he nodded at me, "Beautiful."

My heart jumped at the familiar greeting. I nodded back, "Lord Nathan."

I slipped my arm in his and we all lined up.

"Is she okay?" he asked.

"Just the normal bridal jitters."

We heard the sound of the wedding entrance song begin. They had selected a violin version of "Can't Help Falling in Love."

The doors opened and Jonathan stepped inside with our mothers. I caught a glimpse of the audience, most of who I didn't know. The coordinator was thoughtful enough to seat guests on both sides of the aisle. Nate and I walked in next. As we walked down the aisle, I noticed a big smile on Jonathan and our mother's faces.

Is this what it would have looked like at our wedding?

"Maybe next time," Nate whispered, a soft smile on his face. I looked back confused.

Did I say that out loud?

I walked to my spot at the altar. Nate stood across from me, behind Jonathan.

The rest of the wedding party marched in, the ladies slowly adorning the aisle with white flower petals. The song faded, and everyone stood.

"Canon in D" began to play, and both doors swung open.

There Daniela stood, in all her glory. Her smile soon morphed into raw emotion when she spotted her soon-to-be husband.

Jonathan was also struggling to contain his emotions; Nate comforted him. Gloria and my mom were ugly crying, and I pulled my cotton swab out of my bra to dab my eyes. Her dress sparkled as she walked; The pearls and sequins reflected in the light.

When she finally reached the end, Daniela's cousin stood up and brought a phone to Jonathan. We all looked at each other confused, as this moment was not rehearsed.

"It's for you, Jonathan. Put the phone on speaker."

When Jonathan hesitated, Daniela softly encouraged him. She had to be the mastermind. Jonathan grabbed the phone and placed it on speaker.

"Jonathan?" a heavily accented voice asked.

"Don Julio?" he asked while staring at Daniela. She *would* make him speak to her father at the altar.

"Yeah, Hijo. I'll make this quick. Do you promise to take care of my little girl?" his voice broke as he finished the question.

"Forever, Don Julio," Jonathan responded, never breaking eye contact with Daniela.

"Okay. Then I hand over the responsibility of protecting her, to you," he said before hanging up.

Jonathan took Daniela's hand and helped her climb the altar steps. I held her bouquet and had tissues ready, just in case. Their vows were short and sweet, and after a quick candle lighting cere-mony, it was time to exchange rings. All of a sudden, we heard Gloria shout "Oliver! Ven," and down the aisle he came, with a ring bearer pillow on his back.

I was relieved to see him being a team player, he was not happy the night before.

"Ladies and Gentlemen, I present to you, Mr. and Mrs. Jonathan and Daniela Contreras."

The guests cheered as they shared their first kiss as husband and wife.

12

UNFORGIVEN

Osvaldo gave the girls free touch ups before the wedding photoshoot. I tried to corner him and offered to pay for the extra work.

"If you keep offering me money, I will terminate our friendship, effective immediately," he warned.

"You know how absurd that sounds right?" I laughed.

"Yes, I do."

I gave in and walked him to his car. "Thank you so much for everything. Daniela looks beautiful."

"It was my pleasure, truly." He put his hand on my shoulder. "Now, prepare yourself. I'm about to overstep. That man over there is still in love with you. You and I both know it. You can lie to yourself about your feelings, but it won't do any good. There, I said it." He opened his car door. "We can grab lunch next week. I'll text you!"

He never gave me a chance to reply. It was for the best; I didn't really have a good response.

While the couple took pictures, I noticed my mom and Nate in the distance, walking Oliver. My surprise at seeing them interact quickly died, as I felt another wave of nausea come over me. Eventually, I moved to the far end of a stone ledge to get away from Raquel and Darius; the flirtation between those two was making me cringe.

"Are you feeling okay?" Gloria asked as she approached me.

"I have an upset stomach," I replied, squirming a bit. I felt uncomfortable speaking directly to her. All these years she had been depicted as the Big Bad Wolf, but really, she was just a small, frail, and seemingly kind woman.

She reached into her purse and pulled out a pack of lifesavers. "Have a couple of these. Your sugar might be low."

I thanked her as I popped them into my mouth.

She sighed, "I know my son may have painted me in a bad light over the years. He was right to; I made many mistakes, but I think he and I are moving past that now. My only regret is that it took so long."

I nodded, at a loss for words.

"I won't meddle in your business. But I want you to know he has become a much better communicator over the last few months, and if you find it in your heart to try, you might like what you see . . . I guess that was meddling, huh?"

I laughed. "Kind of, but I take no offense. It's apparent that he's doing better now. I wonder if my absence is the reason . . ."

She shook her head, "Oh no, Emilia. He got better in spite of your absence, not because of it." She patted my thigh, then stood and walked away. My nausea had calmed by then. She may have been right about my sugar.

"Emi!" Raquel shouted as she signaled it was our turn for pictures.

Prior to our entrance into the reception, I pinned Daniela's hair into a low bun and removed her veil so she could dance freely.

The reception began at sunset. I was immensely grateful that they didn't want an elaborate entrance. They selected "If You Love Me" by Melody Gardot, which allowed the wedding party to walk in as they were introduced, as opposed to a high energy dance.

Once the couple was introduced, they swiftly headed to the dance floor. Their first dance was to "Every Time I Close My Eyes" by Babyface featuring Kenny G; an excellent song choice. Watching those two was dreamlike. Jonathan looked at her in amazement; that familiar grin of his showing he had found nirvana. Daniela was beyond radiant.

I realized there was something deep inside me that longed for a moment like that. I had never had regrets about how Nate and I got married, but now, I see the magic behind professing love in the presence of other loved ones—to feel love multiplied.

We were instructed to join the couple for the next song to set the mood and encourage the guests to join in. Nate grabbed my hand and escorted me to the dance floor.

I was flattered by his boldness.

He brought me close, and I could smell his cologne. The scent was unfamiliar to me. It suited him nicely but wasn't something I would have pictured him wearing. I imagined him in a flannel sweater at a deep lake surrounded by pines on a gloomy day. I internally laughed at myself for conjuring up such a cheesy image.

The lights dimmed again, and "My Love" by Lionel Richie came on. It was one of my favorite songs. The lyrics were remarkably simple, yet beautiful.

"Aren't they a little young for Lionel?" I whispered.

"I picked this song," he said. I felt his thumb softly caress the small of my back.

He looked into my eyes, and I felt like I was laid bare. His soft smile always broke through my defenses. This beautiful man felt so strange and new, and I was beyond intrigued, but what could I offer him? I was still a mess, and I couldn't just forget the past twenty years. There were too many emotions to process, and I was in no mental state to handle them.

He leaned in close, pressed his cheek to mine, and softly began to sing the first verse into my ear. It was then I understood why he chose that song.

The lyrics were for me.

My heart dropped to my stomach, and I pressed my forehead into his chest. Instinctively, I wanted to run away. I felt everything —joy, sadness, anger, confusion—and it overwhelmed me.

But I chose to stay. I felt safe again.

As soon as the song ended, he held on to my hand, and after a moment of hesitation, I broke away. We walked back to our table as dinner was being served, and I was grateful that our mothers were seated between us.

My mom leaned over to me and whispered, "You can cut the tension between you two with a knife."

"Mom, drop it," I warned.

My mom ignored me and said, "Raquel, the reception looks amazing!"

She blushed, "I can't take credit for all of it. The Venue took my centerpieces as inspiration and built the rest!"

There were lanterns of all shapes and sizes hanging from the ceiling, and greenery draped along the windows that looked out to the beach. The centerpieces were surrounded by candles and the entire space twinkled. It was classy and elegant, with a touch of boho.

The guests laughed and danced while the bride and groom enjoyed their food. Oliver laid at their feet and chewed on the steak and blueberries he was served.

I managed a few bites before I felt my stomach turn again. My mom noticed my face turning green and accompanied me to the restroom.

"What is wrong with you?" she asked with slight irritation in her voice.

"I don't know, Mom. I've felt off the last couple of weeks. I'm having trouble keeping anything down."

"You didn't sleep with Will, did you? Could you be pregnant?"

I laughed at her ridiculous question. "No, Mom," I sighed. "I never slept with Will."

"Well, go to the doctor, damn it! Get checked out. You can't just continue to get to worse!"

"I know. I will. Go back to the table. I'll be there in a few."

She left in a huff, and I was grateful to have a few minutes to myself.

You can do this, Emilia. One more night, then you can crawl into bed.

I patted my neck with a cold paper towel, then grabbed a mint from the welcome cart. My reflection was concerning. Although

Osvaldo's makeup skills were indeed superior to my under-eye circles, there was nothing he could do about the sadness I saw.

As I stepped out of the bathroom, I noticed a server at the end of the hall. He looked very familiar; very familial. He was tall and lean, with a clean-shaven head and big ears.

He turned to me and smiled, and my heart stopped. I ran back to the reception hall and tried to control my breathing before returning to my seat.

Deep breaths. That was not your father, Emilia.

I got back just in time for the best man speech. Nate delivered a very entertaining account of their childhood. I had heard some of these memories over the years, but they were usually followed by stories of Rick. Jonathan and Daniela got emotional when Nate told the couple he loved them.

Instead of having me speak, we broke tradition and had Daniela's cousin stand in. She worked with her sisters on a surprise video speech, and I was very grateful that Osvaldo had applied three coats of setting spray on her face; she cried that much.

For the mother-son dance, Jonathan chose "Madrecita Querida", a classic ranchera. Daniela, not wanting to miss out, chose a cumbia, "No se Va", to dance with my mom.

The wedding artist I hired unveiled a surprise portrait of the couple's first dance, and their reaction was worth every penny. I watched all the happy people dance and laugh with their loved ones.

Meanwhile, the fog seeped back inside me.

I stepped outside on the back terrace. The night air was brisk and just what I needed. I took a deep breath and closed my eyes.

My eyes stung with unshed frustration. I had to lean on the balcony railing as another dizzy spell came over me.

"Emilia, are you okay?" Nate called behind me.

"I'm fine. I just need a moment." I squeezed my eyes shut but everything continued to spin.

I felt Nate drape my shawl over my shoulders. "We are about to send them off."

"Okay, I'll be right there."

The sendoff was spectacular. Everyone lined up to create a sparkler arch while "Come and Get your Love" by Redbone played. Jonathan and Daniela danced as they got into a black, vintage Chevy Impala with "Just Married" written on the back.

As the guests dispersed, I wished my mom a good night and headed inside to grab my belongings. The groomsmen had already loaded our luggage into Jonathan's car.

I saw Raquel wheeling a wagon with the centerpieces to her trunk. "Flaca, do you need help?" I asked, hoping she'd say no.

"Darius is loading them, then we are headed to a bar," she said, a mischievous twinkle in her eyes. "You get some rest, Sister. You did an amazing job organizing this."

"The weirdest thing happened . . . I thought I saw Dad in there. There was a server who was the same height, had a shaved head, and the same ears."

Raquel nodded. "You're losing it, Emi. Speaking of Dad, I have some items Grandma mailed me. She wanted you to have some of his old belongings and mementos."

I shook my head. "Keep 'em. I don't want them."

She recoiled. "Why not?"

"I don't even have my own place, yet. I don't want to keep accumulating stuff."

"That explains why you don't want them right now. But that's not how you said it."

"Well, that's how I meant it."

Raquel threw her hands up in the air. "Why can't you just admit that you hate him?"

"You mind lowering your voice?" I hissed.

"Yeah, actually, I do mind," she yelled louder. "I am sick of you always shitting all over my dad."

My laugh betrayed the fury that was spreading across my body. "So, how about you stop talking about *your* dad? Ever stop to think that I'm not interested in what you have to say about him?"

"You know what, I will. Forgive me for always expecting you to have some sympathy for a sick person."

"Oh, he was sick, alright."

"Fuck you, Emilia!" she snapped, "you aren't perfect you know. You forget you weren't the only one that dealt with his shit. I watched him destroy my mother. We dealt with his addiction day and night. I didn't have the luxury of going back to my house at the end of the summer."

The remaining guests were now watching us. I was beyond embarrassed. "You must have forgotten yourself. The next time you speak to me like that, we will have a serious problem. I know you've experienced terrible things. I was there for enough of it; I am still haunted by the things I saw him do to our mothers. Your pain, is just as valid as mine, regardless of who had more exposure." I jabbed my finger in her face. "If you choose to forgive him, good for you, I'll recommend you for sainthood. I will not forgive him for the shit he did to me and my mother."

She furiously wiped her tears and got into her car. As she

drove away, I realized it was the first time she and I had ever fought so viciously. I felt awful.

Instead of getting in my own car, I headed to the back terrace.

———

Nate was on the other side of Jonathan's car when he overheard Emilia and Raquel's argument.

When Raquel drove off, Emilia spun around and stormed back into The Venue. She was clearly distressed, and he knew he risked being pushed away again.

She was worth the risk, so he ran after her.

He found her below the terrace on a beach chair, holding her head to her knees.

"Emilia?"

"What?" she mumbled.

"Do you need to see a doctor?"

"Absolutely not!" her head snapped up. "Nate, please just go. I need a moment to think."

"I'm not leaving you."

She laughed; It was sinister. When she looked up, her face showed a plethora of emotion, all at once. He'd never seen this side of her before. He could see her fear. Her grief.

Her anger.

He just wanted to hold her. To tell her that he loved her more than anything. That from the day she entered his life, his days had begun to have meaning; that the dark cloud of fear and pain that had always followed him had subsided, and he wanted to be a better man for her.

"Emilia, honey. Let's just talk. Or you talk, and I'll listen."

"Fine," she mocked, "Let's talk about the irony of what you just said. You aren't leaving? You left me *years* ago."

Nate was dumbfounded. "I'm sorry?"

"I may have walked out five months ago, but you left me years ago. You promised to love me, to take care of me. You were the only person I ever trusted to do that. I got a taste of that in the beginning, then nothing. I was a fly on the fucking wall. When I couldn't provide children, it felt like you gave up on me."

Her sobs grew in intensity. He wanted to pick her up in his arms and soothe her, but he knew better; she would scold him, like she always did.

"I'm sorry I couldn't give you children, Nate. I tried . . . I tried so hard."

Her anguished cries were tearing at his soul. "Baby, I never faulted you for the miscarriages. I was never angry. Sad, of course, because I hated seeing you grieve like that. And when I tried to be there for you, you didn't want to hear it. Eventually, I gave up trying to be vulnerable, and for that I'm so sorry, Em."

He inched closer to her. She held herself as she cried, the moon's silver light shining on her tear-stricken face.

"I'm sorry that I checked out emotionally."

"I don't understand why?" her sad eyes fixed on him in a piercing stare.

He hesitated, and his breath caught. Fighting back his own tears, he mustered as gently as he could. "Because when I tried to be there for you, I felt ridiculed. It reminded me of my mom. I felt I was made to feel stupid for trying to comfort you. It didn't feel safe to show my emotions around you anymore."

"What are you talking about, I ne—"

"Emilia," he said gently, "think back, please. I'm not making this shit up."

Her brows furrowed as she processed what he was saying, as if sifting through a mental rolodex for evidence of his claims.

After a moment, she swallowed. "I'm sorry for doing that to you. I don't know how to handle emotion when heavy shit happens. Half the time I can't even perceive whether I am feeling anything. I didn't realize I was making you feel that way. I guess, subconsciously, I just didn't want to have to process it myself."

Nate knelt in front of her. "I know that now, Baby. I was so caught up in my own pain, I didn't realize you were struggling to cope as well." He brushed her tears away, then cupped her face. "I promise you this. I've never stopped loving you. I've never thought less of you. You are the woman I continue to dream about."

She leaned into his hand, and he noticed her tremble. "You're freezing, Emilia. Let's go inside, okay?"

She shook her head. "No, the air soothes my nausea."

"Okay, well Jonathan has a blanket in his car. I'll be right back."

He hurried to the car, excitement building in his gut. He hoped they had reached a breakthrough and could at least talk through some of their issues.

Maybe, just maybe, he could get his wife back.

As Nathan returned to the beach chair, he noticed it was empty. He looked around and spotted a figure running full speed toward the trees at the end of the beach. "Emilia!" he shouted, panic coming over him. He took off his shoes and ran after her into the woods.

I was still reeling from everything Nate had just confessed. Him shedding light on what happened all those years ago helped everything click into place. His distance, my resentment, and how they became entangled over the years was a result of poor communication.

It was, again, too much to process for one night, but oddly, I felt a little lighter.

There was a noise over my shoulder. I figured it was Nate returning with the blanket. I looked to my left. That's when I saw the server walking toward the beach at a brisk pace.

I shot up. As soon as I called out to him, he broke into a run. Unable to control my impulse, I chased after him. I needed to clear any lingering doubt that it was my father. After all, I never actually saw his body. What if it was a mistake, and he was actually alive?

I thought I heard someone call my name behind me, but I wouldn't let up.

He was running incredibly fast, even through the trees. I felt the rocks and branches dig into my feet, but it didn't slow me down.

As soon as I entered the cove, I felt a wave of pressure release in my head. Skies were clear, and the full moon illuminated the beach. The server sat upright on one of the logs and I slowed down so he wouldn't run off again. As I reached him, I felt another wave of dizziness wash over me. Before I could right myself, I fell backward. But I didn't land.

I just kept falling into the darkness.

The marble reflection leaves me speechless. I am ten years old again. French braids frame my youthful face, and my overalls look brand new. My father is still beaming, but I am mortified.

I storm past him. I don't care where we are anymore. I just need to go home.

As soon as I cross the threshold between the house and outside, the skies turn upside down and everything blurs.

Then I stand at a stormy shore. It's the hidey spot.

Except, something is wrong. I've never seen the cove like this before. The ocean is enraged. The marine-blue waters are now an icy sage. The once peaceful atmosphere feels like it is being suctioned out by an invisible force. It is so hard to breathe here. Waves are crashing against the rocks with a violent fervor.

The outer edges of the sky are almost black, as if swallowing the aqua sky whole. Even the tree where I sought refuge is . . . otherworldly. Leaves on one side glow like fire, their amber leaves flying into the ocean, incinerating as soon as they touch the water.

The other side is in full bloom, its blossoms a gradient shade of teal and lilac.

"This is all yours, Hija," he utters behind me.

I spin around, staring at him, confused, scared . . .

Angry.

"Why. Are. We. Here, Pablo?" I bite.

"Because, you have something to say."

"I have nothing to say to you," I spit.

His gentle smile confuses me all the more, and my heart grows with rage. Just then, lightning whips through the sky and I jump.

"You have a lot to say to me."

"You aren't real!" I shout. "This is just another dream. I'm sick and tired of dreaming of you. Every night, the memories come back. Every night, you beat me, and scream at me, and torment me. I want you gone."

He nods.

"Why are you nodding?" I ask, my hands balling into fists.

"I have been on your mind a lot."

"Why? I scream. "Why am I wearing these stupid, fucking clothes. The last time I wore this, you beat me senseless over something I didn't even do! What do you want from me? I don't want to talk to you. You were cruel to everyone around you. All you ever thought about was yourself!"

The tears sting as they trail down my face. They feel like cactus pricks slicing at my cheeks. The faster they come down, the harder it rains.

He is calm. I don't understand why I am falling apart and he is serene.

"You tell me, Emilia. Why do you think about me?"

"I don't choose to think about you. You torment me! You were a terrible father," I gasp as the pain forces itself out, "and you were an awful husband. Yet, somehow, Marta, Grandma, Raquel, even Mom, forgave you. Well guess what? I don't. I had to turn off all my emotions around you because there was no room for anyone else. I wasn't allowed to be scared, or sad, or angry, without severe consequence."

He nods, his smile gone, and a focused expression in its place.

"Why couldn't you just . . . be there for me?" I sob. "I didn't ask to be born. I see parents—fathers—love and encourage their daughters, teach them how special they are. I've only known the opposite. You just had to be there, Papi, to teach me and guide me. I'm not a hard person to love. At least, I wasn't. Now I'm this incredible mess, and don't even know how to pick up the pieces."

"I was diseased."

"You could have tried to get better. I was worth a shot. Raquel was worth a shot. Look at her, she witnessed terrible things, but with just crumbs more than you gave me, she reveres you. You could have tried, but instead you chose to blame everyone else for your pain."

"You're right," he says.

"What?" I ask, stunned.

He smiles. "I never knew how to properly deal with my emotions. I chose destruction. I was not a good father, son, or husband. You are right."

"So, what?" I feel smoke coming out of my ears; the sky turns crimson. "You admit you were wrong, and I'm just supposed to let it go?"

"No. You simply let it go."

"Excuse me?" I scream, ready to pounce.

"Hija, I live in your past. I exist only in your memory. I caused you so much pain, and I taught you how to bottle it up. You have been cut off from your emotions for so long, but it's time to wake up."

"Wake up?" I ask, confused. I feel my shoulders shake.

"Emilia!" it sounds like Nate's voice, "Baby, please wake up!"

13

DETENTE

The episode at the beach landed me in the hospital. The last time I was in an emergency room, I had suffered my final miscarriage. I detested the smell, the sounds, the bright lights; everything reminded me of those fateful trips.

In that moment, I couldn't handle how sweet and attentive Nate was being, so I called my mom to come stay with me instead. He appeared hurt at my sending him home but didn't argue. He gave me a kiss on the forehead and told me to call him if I needed anything.

The doctor said I was dehydrated, but otherwise fine. I didn't mention the dreams, or the man I saw at the cove for fear of being held for psychiatric evaluation. After receiving electrolytes, I was discharged, and my mom insisted I stay with her for a couple of days.

I took a shower, climbed into bed, and didn't wake up for almost two days.

I finally stirred when I felt my mom's fingers on my wrist. She told me she would come in throughout the day to make sure I was still breathing. Nate called my mom constantly to check up on me. She called Sage on my behalf to let her know I wouldn't be back to the house for a few days.

She came in again with a piping hot bowl of sopa de fideo.

"Ven, Hija. You need sustenance."

I sat up in bed as she placed a tray on my lap; it smelled so good. The first bite dropped down to my stomach like a ton of bricks, but soon after I became ravenous.

"What happened out there, Emilia?" she asked softly.

"I thought I saw someone that looked like my father walking on the beach. When I called out to him, he began to run toward the cove, and something told me to follow him. When I caught up to him, I guess I passed out."

"Why would you run after a stranger alone, at a strange beach?"

I thought about it for a second, then shrugged. "I honestly don't know. I wasn't thinking. But if it's any consolation, it's not a strange beach. I'm very familiar with the cove just beyond the trees."

"It's not. That was reckless and dangerous. I'd never seen Nate look so scared . . ."

"I know, Mom."

She paused, then looked up at me. "Did you see the man when you cleared the woods?"

"Yes, he was sitting on one of the logs. Did Nate see him?"

"No, Mija, no one was there."

"Nate must not have noticed him. I'm not crazy, Mom. I saw him."

"If you say so . . ." she said as she took my tray over to the dresser.

Catching up on sleep had done wonders for my headspace. Although there was still a lot to process, I realized I wasn't going to get better if I didn't start getting things off my chest. My talk with Nate was incredibly cathartic. I realized in that moment, that I had a few things to say to my mother as well.

"Mami, may I ask you something?"

"Hmm?"

"Please don't take this the wrong way . . . I don't blame you for the things my father did. But, knowing how violent he was, why did you still send me to his house every summer?"

She sighed. "Because everyone lied to me. Your grandmother told me he was clean. Marta always vouched for him when I'd ask how he was treating you. I'd even ask you how your summer was, and you'd say it was fine. Deep down, I wanted to believe it so you could have a relationship with him, but I should have known better."

I felt the emotion bubble up inside me again. "What about those times I'd call you crying, saying I wanted to come home?"

Her sad eyes met mine. "I chose to listen to the adults. They said you were unhappy because you didn't get your way. They told me they spanked you for misbehaving. I regret not believing you more."

"I was not 'spanked,' Mom. I was beaten."

She scoffed. "Emilia, you were not beaten, don't exaggerate."

The urge to lash out was great. I didn't have the energy to fight, but I would not allow her to sweep my pain under the rug.

I did enough of that myself.

"He beat me, Mom. And so did you. The way you both hit

me . . . was wrong. It never felt like I was being disciplined or corrected; there was a rage inside both of you, and I felt like the whipping post where you would release your anger."

Her lips quivered. "I never meant to be cruel, Emilia. We were disciplined so much worse in our country. What wasn't I hit with? Switches, cords, belts, shoes, smacks across the face, being dragged by my hair, pulled by the ear, you name it. I am not trying to make excuses here. It was just . . . the only way I knew."

Wiping my tears, I nodded. "I understand, Mami. But it doesn't change where I am now. Something inside me broke all those years ago. It wasn't until very recently that I accepted how much my father affected me. How much you affected me."

I took her hand in mine. She was trembling, and I realized I had hit a sore spot for her as well. "I also want you to know, that I remember all the back-to-back shifts, the clean house, the home cooked meals. I remember how hard you tried to give me a decent life, Mom."

We held each other as we cried. The weight in my chest began to lighten.

I called Nate to thank him for taking care of me. He was relieved to hear I was doing better, and I could tell he wanted to pick up our conversation from that evening, but I wasn't ready. He flew back to North Carolina, but offered to meet me whenever I was ready to talk.

Shortly after that conversation, Raquel sent a very curt text letting me know my grandmother had fallen ill. I agreed to meet her at my grandmother's house which was a few hours away.

Although I felt anxiety around going back to "the house of horrors," I persisted.

Raquel did not tell her I was coming, so when I walked through the door, both she and Sara were stunned. I had not set foot in that house in more than two decades. I was pleasantly surprised to see new living room furniture and that the walls had been painted; it felt less like a trip in a time machine.

Sara didn't appear bothered that I came.

In fact, she looked . . . happy.

Raquel avoided eye contact with me and went into the kitchen. I spotted the dining table in the corner. The same dining table where Marta used to sit and watch for my father.

"You came just in time! Raquel is making enchiladas de carne!" my grandmother said.

I noticed she was hooked up to an oxygen tank. Sara told me she had been fighting pneumonia for a few weeks.

"Did you like the items I sent you?" she asked in between coughs.

"I haven't given her the box yet, Abuela. I keep forgetting," Raquel lied from the kitchen. I appreciated her covering for me, although I suspected it was more for my grandmother's benefit.

"Ah, okay. No worries. It was just a few things your dad used to keep tucked away in his closet. But! I was in such a rush to get to the post office, I left something very special out."

She reached behind her recliner and pulled a photo album from her bookcase. "This is yours."

The pink and white photo album was very old. It was clearly an eighties relic, with its fabric exterior and ribbon tie. I opened it and my jaw dropped.

The first picture was of a very young man with tan skin, a

mullet, and big ears, laying on a bed, feeding his baby a bottle. The next was the same young man at a beach, carrying a tricycle and unicorn floatie while his young toddler stood for a picture. There were pictures of all stages of my life, some with my grandmother, some with my father, some with Raquel.

There was laughter. All those happy memories, but I hadn't remembered any of them. They slowly emerged as I studied the pictures; they must've been hidden behind the shadows.

"I was going to give you this album as a graduation present, but you ran off and got married," she laughed. "I know your father wasn't perfect, Emilia. Far from it. He did a lot of horrible things. But I loved my son, and I know he loved his daughters."

I wrapped my arms around my grandmother. Then we all sat at the dining table and enjoyed dinner together.

After saying my goodbyes, Raquel walked me to my car. She wasn't avoiding me anymore, but I could tell she was still upset. I figured I'd done enough damage the week before and let her drive the conversation.

"Let me give you this, before I forget." She opened her trunk and pulled out an old shoebox. "Just open it, Emi. You'll be surprised at what you find." She hugged me tight.

I promised her I would, then got in my car. When I saw her go back inside, I opened the box.

Inside was a worn romance novella and a manila envelope. It contained a certified copy of my birth certificate, a photocopy of my first passport, and a hospital announcement that read "HAPPY BIRTHDAY, EMILIA SALINAS! 7LBS 1OZ." and had my baby footprints. He saved all his custody orders, my old report cards, and honor roll certificates. Under the envelope, I found a pair of baby socks with pink ruffles, and a baby bracelet with my name.

I let out the ugliest cry I'd ever heard.

Pain swept over me like torrential rain. I wept as I gripped those little socks in my balled fists.

For the first time in my life, I woefully mourned the father I never knew.

As if three emotionally charged events weren't enough, I quickly ushered in another.

Andy called me to catch up and asked if I wanted to stop by Fire Sign to check out the new shipment of crystals she had received. I agreed to take a peek, as Sage's birthday was quickly approaching, and I wanted to get a Selenite tower for her fireplace.

When I arrived, however, I quickly realized I was being ambushed. Will stood at the register with his mom, looking as delicious as ever. His bright smile widened when he saw me. I smiled back and gave him a big hug.

The energy felt very different this time; I expected an awkward reunion, but it felt like hugging an old friend. Andy was her bright, energetic self, and conversation was easy. After purchasing the tower, Will offered to buy me a cup of coffee.

We walked to the coffee shop down the street, and he filled me in on everything I'd missed over the past month, and I told him about my recent troubles.

"I am on the mend, though." I reassured him.

"And beautiful as ever, Emilia. Don't ever forget that. I meant what I said, you deserve the world."

After a last embrace, we agreed to meet again at the next shindig.

It turned out that the next shindig was a few days later. When Sage returned, Andy and Will threw her a surprise welcome/birthday party at a local pub. Sage was effervescent as always, and it was clear that she was the glue that brought all of us together.

During Karaoke hour, Osvaldo and I were chosen to be backup singers for Andy while she wailed to "Proud Mary." Osvaldo had to carry me off the stage, I was laughing so hard.

Sage danced, cried, and vibed the whole evening. I met more of her friends and some of her family. But the highlight of the party was her speech.

"So many friends and family here tonight. Every one of you have told me at some point how much I mean to you. Now it's my turn. I ask the universe to show me beauty every day. And every day, I get to see it. But on extra special days, it brings me people like you! Thank you for being true friends. It is an honor to just be with you."

There wasn't a dry eye in the room.

After the party wrapped up, she and I headed home, but I could tell she was still high on love, so I made a small detour. "Shall we go to the hidey spot?"

She squealed as I turned into the park.

It was my first time coming to the hidey spot at sunset; I usually only ever saw it at night or just before dawn. I hadn't thought it could get anymore magical.

I was wrong.

Pink hues splattered across the sky; it brought with it a warm and silky feeling. I felt as if the beach was wrapping us up in love.

The beech tree hovered over us like a canopy of colors. She and I sat on a log and watched the waves as she told me stories of her trip.

"My grandparents finally agreed to come live with me!" she cheered.

"That's so exciting, Sage!"

"Tell me, how are you sleeping?"

"A lot better now. I've been having some heavy conversations with my family. I didn't realize I was carrying so much . . . until the night of the wedding."

"It sounds like a rollercoaster of emotions with Raquel, Nathan, and Daniela," she added.

"And my father."

"Oh?" she asked, confused.

I let her in on my little secret. I remembered everything I said to my father while unconscious that night. She listened intently as I recounted my conversation with him. When I finished, her mouth was agape.

"You must think I'm crazy . . ."

"No. Not one bit," she said looking around. "This place really is magical . . . I am beyond humbled that it gave you a place to lay down your grief."

I smiled. "Me too."

"So . . ." she asked bashfully, "what about Nathan?"

I frowned. "I've made a decision about him too."

Three weeks had passed with no word from Emilia. Nate tried to focus on the progress he'd made with his family and not let her silence discourage him. Instead, he devoted his attention to packing up the house and preparing for his move.

He put in his notice at work and decided he would look for new job opportunities that aligned with his passions. He had yet to revisit where his passions lay at this stage in his life, but he figured there was plenty of time to find out.

He was just about to hop in the shower when he heard the doorbell ring. He swung the front door open expecting his grocery delivery, but there was no one there. He checked for the groceries at the side door, and when he didn't see anyone, stepped back inside and headed upstairs to the bathroom. Just as he turned the water on, the doorbell rang again.

Then again. And again. And again.

He spun around and marched down the stairs, quickly becoming irritated.

When he opened the door, he saw Emilia with a backpack over her shoulder, her finger hovering over the doorbell. Before she got a chance to speak, he engulfed her.

She melted into his embrace, and they cried.

His wife was home.

He carried her to the couch and held her, without saying a word. After a while, she asked, "Where is this kitty of yours?"

"Capri!" he called out. Emilia's body stiffened.

"What did you just call her?" she whispered. Just then, Capri sauntered over and without hesitation, jumped onto her lap. She looked into Emilia's eyes, then nuzzled her chin. Emilia burst into tears and cradled her new cat.

"You're not mad about the name?" Nate asked. Emilia shook her head and smiled. "I'm sorry you had to wait so long out there. I was about to jump in the shower."

"I didn't wait at all." she replied, "You opened the door before I had a chance to ring the doorbell."

Nate was puzzled. "I thought I heard the—never mind . . . I'm just glad you're here."

"Are you remodeling?" she asked as she looked around at all the boxes.

"I listed the house, Baby . . ."

Her eyes widened.

"I was going to downsize for a bit, then move wherever I find a job."

"You left your job?"

He laughed, "There is a lot to catch you up on, but first, are you here to stay?"

"No."

Nate frowned.

"I'm here to collect you. I wanted to go back home, but come to find out, you are my home. So, I'm bringing you home . . . to our hometown . . . am I making sense?"

"Sure..." he chuckled, unable to contain his joy. He brought Emilia's face to his and kissed her hard. He had longed for the opportunity from the moment he saw her at the rehearsal dinner. Her soft lips felt so smooth, and he never wanted to let go. When she broke away, she whispered, "I love you, Nate."

He whispered back, "Forever, Beautiful."

EPILOGUE

"It is such a pleasure to finally meet you, Emilia," Ann smiled.

She studied the couple whose fingers were interlaced on the couch. Nate's bright smile was all the confirmation she needed.

Reconciliation never looked so good.

When Nate called to schedule a couple's session, Ann offered to see them the next morning. She lied about having an opening; it was her day off. She would never admit it to Nate, but she had grown a soft spot for him over the years and was excited to finally see him on an upward path.

"It's nice to meet you too, Ann. Thank you for seeing us on such short notice." Emilia smiled at Nate, "I'll admit, I'm a tad nervous. This is my first ever therapy session."

They began with a detailed account of the events that occurred in New York, followed by Emilia's return to North Carolina. They had decided to reconcile and listed their house for sale.

"We are relocating to Long Island." Nate's eyes brightened,

"We both want to be closer to family and . . . I plan to take the Bar exam."

"That's excellent news, Nathan!" Ann smiled proudly.

"It's a shame we can't take you with us," Nate confessed.

"I offer virtual sessions, if you'd like to continue working together?"

"Absolutely!" they said in unison.

After Emilia shared some of her background, Ann recommended individual counseling to address her personal trauma. They agreed to weekly couple's therapy for a few months, then, as needed.

When the happy couple left, Ann added her notes to Nate's file, but instead of placing it on her desk with the rest of her regular clients, she filed it away in her patient cabinet.

That action made her smile.

Nate lazily ran his fingers through my hair as I rested on him. Capri's light purrs tickled my stomach; it was her favorite spot to nap. Ever since I arrived, she had been stuck to me like glue, and only paid attention to Nate when it was playtime. Instead of watching TV like I used to, I'd decided to spend my quiet time reading.

I'd committed to pursuing new interests upon our return to New York. Sage had just completed renovations on a house a few blocks from her and offered to lease it to us for a year, while we settled in.

Between the freelance gigs with Osvaldo and helping Raquel revamp her jewelry business, I planned to take piano lessons and a photography course. I didn't want to waste another moment and thought the photography skills would come in handy as I documented our new life.

Nate was excited to take the Bar and spend more time with his family. I was ready to support him any way I could. We were also thrilled about the opportunity to dote on Jonathan and Daniela's children; they wanted five kids and planned to start right away.

I broke away from my book to admire the painting on the wall. To my surprise, Nate had commissioned the artist at the wedding reception to take a picture of us while we danced, then draw a portrait. When I walked into our bedroom and saw it, I burst into tears . . . again.

I felt an immense warmth in my heart. My mind didn't race as much or as often, although it did happen from time to time. When the emotions came, I didn't push them down, or berate myself for feeling them; I just let them flow on by.

"I love you" by the Bees played softly on the sound bar as I felt my eyelids grow heavy. Right before drifting off, I heard my husband whisper, "Get some sleep, Baby. I got you."

———

A calm summer breeze caresses my face as my eyes open. I find myself swinging on a hammock beneath a set of palm trees. The pillowy clouds drift gently across a crystal-clear sky. I sit up and admire the warm tropical ocean; the waves sparkle as they roll onto the shore.

Laughter breaks out and I turn around. In the distance, a man chases a child around a large sandcastle. Two other children squeal as the man catches the third and swings him in the air.

After a moment, he looks up at me and waves. I wave back, unable to recognize him from afar. He sets the child down, then walks to a set of beach chairs on the shoreline; the kids continue to play in the sand.

I recognize him as soon as I draw closer. My father writes something in the sand, then sits down in his large chair with a worn romance novella in hand.

"¡Amor!" he exclaims. His olive skin glistens in the sun. He radiates a peacefulness beyond words.

I sigh.

My once hardy exterior, the one that protected me all those years, is no more. When I see my father, pain is no longer the immediate reaction. He is no longer a monster. He is just my dad. I realize that regardless of whether his love for me was enough, *my* love for me is *more* than enough.

"Hi, Papi." I smile and sit beside him.

"You're early, Hija, but I'm glad you came."

I nod. "I can't seem to control my timing."

He chuckles. "Not true. You came because you were ready."

Just then, a little girl runs up to me. She takes my palm and turns it face up, then places a seashell in it. Her smile is so familiar. It reminds me of Nate and Jonathan. She giggles, then runs off.

My dad smiles as he keeps reading his novella.

"I think I know why I came."

He sets his book down and turns to me, a warm smile inviting me to elaborate.

"It's to tell you that I'm ready to move on. I spent years downplaying the trauma I experienced at your hands, convincing myself it was no big deal; that I had overcome the pain you caused. All I really did was take the weight of my hurt and tie it around my waist, where it was more comfortable to carry. Where I didn't have to acknowledge it was dragging behind me."

I wipe the tears that slowly trail down my cheeks, admiring how they glisten in the sunlight. "When the triggers come, I will remind myself that I can handle the emotions, whether good or bad. I will absorb the cost of forgiving you, because the cycle ends here."

He smiles wide, then grabs a hold of my hand. A burst of energy fills me, and I notice how much my hand resembles his.

Two little boys run up to him and hug his legs. He whispers in their ear, and they each take one of my hands, then place a seashell in my palm. Their warm brown eyes almost glow.

We stand and watch them run back to the sandcastle.

"Who are those kids, Papi?"

You know who they are . . .

I smile, confused, then do a double take. The words choke on each other as my breath catches in my throat. Tears rush from my eyes. "Are those my—"

"They are well taken care of, Emilia. You have my word. We will be here until you are ready."

I look on in awe. It all makes sense now.

They look so much like their daddy, and I only wish I could give Nate a peek into what I am witnessing. My dad and I walk over and play with them for a while. I try to memorize the sound of their laughter and study their features, so that I never forget.

The missing pieces of my heart rest here.

In my own little hidey spot.

As the sun begins to set, they run inside the house, where a woman greets them. She looks over at me and waves. Before I could ask who it is, he grabs my hand and walks me closer to the shoreline.

"Look at the writing," he whispers.

It reads—FORGIVEN

"Is that a question or statement?" I ask.

"You tell me," he smiles.

I grab a nearby branch and rewrite—UNFORGIVEN

"There we go," I declare.

He looks up at me, his confused expression making me smile.

"You're unforgiven, Dad," I explain as I grab his hand.

"Understood and forgiven."

The End

ACKNOWLEDGMENTS

To my husband. O, your unwavering love and support deserves more than mere words of gratitude, but they are a good start. Thank you for reminding me of my potential all the way to the end. I love you.

To my gracious beta readers, Brittany and Gerrick. I will never forget the late-night zoom calls after a long day of work and responsibilities. The months of laughter and creativity have become core memories, and I am eternally grateful for your help getting this project off the ground.

To @firefly.bookcover.designer, thank you for helping me bring that fateful beach scene to life, long before I wrote it...

To @simplyspellboundedits, you treated this story with so much care, and your editing skills are divine.

And lastly...

To my father.

You are forgiven.

READY FOR MORE?

The second installment in the Unforgiven series, Acritud, will be released in 2024. Here's a sneak peek:

Stefany is a renowned immigration attorney, known for having a fierce conviction to protect her client's rights and secure their futures. However, beneath her composed exterior lies a deep-seated anger that is growing increasingly difficult to manage. As she navigates the complex world of immigration law, each case she takes on stokes her anger, a constant reminder of the systemic flaws and how countless lives are affected by them. Through the flames, she finds herself unexpectedly drawn to a mutual friend, Will, a compassionate and understanding individual with a pestering habit of seeing right past her tough exterior.

While Stefany fights for justice in the courtroom, she must also confront her own inner demons. As she delves into her past and confronts her own personal struggles, Stefany must learn to let go of her anger and allow herself the chance at happiness, and the possibility... of romance.